THE
RED
SPY

THE
RED
SPY

ABHISHEK SRIVASTAVA

Srishti
PUBLISHERS & DISTRIBUTORS

SRISHTI PUBLISHERS & DISTRIBUTORS
Registered Office: N-16, C.R. Park
New Delhi – 110 019
Corporate Office: 212A, Peacock Lane
Shahpur Jat, New Delhi – 110 049
editorial@srishtipublishers.com

First published by
Srishti Publishers & Distributors in 2019

Copyright © Abhishek Srivastava, 2019

10 9 8 7 6 5 4 3 2 1

Dedicated to,

Kautilya's samsthas and sancaras,

who live by the code **धर्मोरक्षतिरक्षितः**

(The law protects when it is protected)

and

www.google.com.

Acknowledgements

Deveshwar Dayal and Shweta Bharti: The day I thought of writing the novel, until the day I finished the first draft, subconsciously all I ever wanted was to impress you guys with my writing. I hope I have lived up to your expectations. This novel gave me a remarkable opportunity to dive into the imaginative world of mine. But whenever I sank too deep and lost a step, you pulled me out of the uncertainty and put me back on track. This novel will be a living monument of our brotherhood. Cheers! Your better half, Shweta, has also played a special role in my journey. People often do not realize how their thoughtful act can change someone's narrative. Without realizing, she did the same when she read the first draft, clearly pointing out that I have an imaginative prowess. Being an editor herself, her remarks changed the course of my life. Thank you and a big hug to your wonderful togetherness.

Suhail Mathur, my literary agent, a man with a promise, and a thorough gentleman. Without you, my novel would never have seen the light of the day. You and The Book Bakers made a promise to a newcomer like me, and ensured that I lived my dream.

Team Srishti Publishers and Arup Bose, the publisher: Thank you for believing in me and my story. Stuti, my editor – appreciate your dedication for adding the extra shine to my novel.

My mother, my elixir of life: You ensured proper resources for a Hindi medium boy to learn to speak and write in English. Trust me, one of the reasons I wrote this novel is to demonstrate that your efforts did not go in vain.

My "Ardhangini" Puja: Your smile of a thousand suns has been lighting up each day of my life. Your happy-go-lucky attitude empowers me every second. You complete me, my love.

Aalya, my daughter, my blessing and my pride: Now that you can read and write, your little queries about the novel make me proud of my deeds.

Vivek and Dipak, my constant companions: If I had asked for the moon, I am sure you guys would have fetched it for me! Thanks for allowing me to spend the most precious moments of my life with you.

Sanju Manoharlal Panjabi, Sambit Chandran Dash, and Rajeev Ranjan: You all continue to inspire me. You taught me to be professional and stay humble at the same time.

Dipankar, Shakil, Abhinav, Jayanto, Sanjay, Vikram, Arun, Vikas, Basu, Deep, Kamal, Digvijay, Virendra, Varsha, Roshni, Vishal and Victor Daju: Your friendship means the most to me.

Papa: At times, there are certain things that you regret all your life. Mine was that I never showed my father how much I loved him, at least not enough. I have lost my chance now. My mentor, my friend, and my teacher, I know you are watching me from wherever you are. I love you dearly.

Lord Shiva - Sovereign of the origin, position, and destruction of the universe is Shiva. Sat-Sat Naman.

A note from the author

Red is the colour of extremes. It's the colour of seduction, violence, anger, danger, war, strength, determination, passion, as well as love. Our ancestors saw red as the colour of blood – energy and primal life forces.

I intend to use the colour's symbolism to impart a deeper meaning to the words and to transform the written content into a powerful instrument.

The Red, the White, and the Dark: My starting the story with these colours suggests that you should anticipate that characters in the novel will change their colours as the story progresses, and the characters will evolve from being White (Saint) to Dark (Satan).

In the game of chess, the White and the Dark wage war against each other. Red is the price they pay. But what if Red is not the price? What if Red is the actual perpetrator?

Prologue

Somewhere in Turkey

Aman was roughly dragged by two men into that very masculine chamber that smelled of Moroccan pipe tobacco – *shisha*. He was turned around and made to sit on a chair by his captors before the shroud covering him was removed. His eyes adjusted to the glaring white light of the halogen light. He wanted to rub his eyes for some comfort, but his hands were chained to the steel chair drilled into the floor. He knew his interrogation had just started. No matter how well trained you are for such interrogations, the reality is always harsh. He realized that from then on his every breath would be as painful as the last one. Before this terror could damage his spirit, he closed his eyes and remembered the moment in the Army when he was awarded the national emblem – it proved his love for his country and vice versa.

"Lovers united!" A firm voice confirmed him of his actual captor. A man with a bony face covered in a beard and a moustache. He was wearing a white suit with a yellow shirt and a matching tie. As soon as he entered, he ordered the lights to be dimmed. He immediately recognized the man as Jan

Mohammad Baloch, a.k.a Mir, his incarcerator. Then he saw the person standing next to Mir. He had never imagined this.

"Leave her, you bastard!" the chained man shouted in frustration.

"Do you really think I have my entire day reserved for you? Everybody has a breaking point!"

The chained figure knew that the odds were not in his favour and Mir was not in a mood to negotiate. The thought gave him a chill. He realized that this was going to be a quick and ruthless interrogation. *Answer and die! Suffer, answer and die!*

To add to his misery, after a while, his captor made his point clear by punching his partner hard on the stomach. She fell to her knees and then on to the floor, as blood spurted from her mouth.

Mir walked behind him and rested his hand on him; it was a very unusual touch to experience. He spoke softly, "Hopeless, you Indian bastard!"

"I have a duty to my country which supersedes any other considerations, and that includes any revulsion I may feel towards you. Today you may believe that you have an upper hand in this game, but let me assure you, if you harm her in any way, then you will learn exactly what kind of a bastard I can be," the chained man responded, giving his captor a chill at first, then angering him instead.

The bony face came rushing down in his face and grabbed his neck, punching him repeatedly, making his nose bleed. He grunted with pain.

"You pathetic Indian, let me be clear what I am going to do next. My men are going to enjoy her to the fullest and then I am going to kill her in front of you and show you what I am capable of!

"The only thing you can do now is tell me whatever you know about 'Operation Changez'."

"I have no idea what you are talking about, and even if I did, do you reckon that I am just going to spell it out for you?" the chained man said.

"Thank you for being very clear."

Mir's men rushed towards her like mad dogs. She put up a brave fight, but they outnumbered her. She was wounded first, and then, when she couldn't fight anymore, they put her on a table, chained her and made her face her companion. She was losing blood; her time was near, but they showed no mercy. One of the leaders from the pack shouted, "Last chance!"

However, there came no reply.

They began their heinous act. She was in her senses, but couldn't move or be rescued. He watched it all with a stone face, his eyes red with agony. She had tears rolling down her cheeks and tried to move her face to the other side. She felt more betrayed than naked, watching him in the eye. But they made sure that she couldn't.

It went on for almost an hour, all three of them taking turns in raping her. When they were done, she was left with a few breaths in her body.

"Shame! Such a shame!" Mir emerged from the dark corner. "Anything you wish to share about Changez?"

The man did not respond.

"Gee... what happened to an Indian tiger? Did he lose his balls? Did you dogs cut them too?" The leader of the pack

– Bulla 'The Butcher' – made a gesture, followed by wild laughter.

They slid the table and put the naked, bleeding, half-dead girl in front of him.

And then Mir spoke in an animated tone, "Do her a favour and spill the truth… what… do… you know about… Operation Changez?"

The man raised his head; his eyes were bloodshot and red. But not a word.

Mir lost his patience, drew out his gun and pointed it towards her temple.

"Please… tell him…" She was filled with pain and misery; her broken voice pleading to her superior to save her life.

The man looked at her with broken, soulless eyes and tilted his head down. With shame? Agony? Who knew for sure? There was silence for a moment, and then came the deadly sound of gunfire. A fragment of her temple blew off amid a ghastly spray of blood, instantly declaring her dead.

After a pause, the man murmured, "I therefore commit Zehana to the ground; earth to earth, ashes to ashes, dust to dust; in the sure and certain hope of the resurrection from her miserable life."

One

The Red, the White
and the Dark

Eastern Pakistan
3 November 1971

An abandoned cottage lay amidst the small pine forest near Nawabganj district. The single lantern burning at its doorstep was the only sign of life inside the house.

Inside the cottage sat a man on the wooden armchair, quite uncertain of his situation. He had a calm and composed look masking the anxiety within. He was surrounded by a group of five men. This man on the chair was Khurshid A. Niazi, the unified commander of the Eastern Military High Command of the Pakistan Armed Forces. He also was a father to a six-month-old baby and husband to a loving wife. Those being the very reasons that he was unable to look at the photographs scattered on the table. Now he knew exactly why he was asked to meet in the cottage without his personal guards. The man sitting opposite him shot him a straight question,

"How would you like me to proceed further, Niazi Sahib, like this... or this? If I were to choose, I would go by this!" and he threw some more black and white photographs at the table, above the previous ones.

Without realizing, Niazi found himself on his knees, pleading to these men. He didn't know how to react to the questions posed by this man.

From the moment he received the letter, he knew something was wrong, but not even once did the thought cross his mind that these bastards, Indians, would go to the extent of kidnapping his family. That his own tactics could entrap him someday was beyond his wildest imagination. Inside his territory, he was the king, but this was not his turf. Looking at his wife and only child's photographs being held captive by these men or their organization, brought him to his knees for the first time in his life. His eyes watered and blurred his vision as each photograph showed the most brutal form of violence – beheaded children and carved out women, the same age as his wife and his child.

One of the men, in a black suit and thick black transparent plastic glasses, R.K. Rao – Chief of RAW, took control of this dishonourable meeting comprising two senior-most officials of eastern Pakistan armed forces, Niazi and his deputy Shariff Mohammad, N.K. Osmani, Commander-in-Chief of Mukti Bahini and two men in identical suits guarding Chief of RAW.

Rao spoke again in a cold voice, "Niazi Sahib, don't worry. My orders are clear. I cannot harm your family. You don't have any other choice but to betray your country." Niazi understood that Rao clearly knew his position and meant business. Shariff, the deputy to Niazi, argued, "It's inhuman to do such a bloody act to just win this war; have your balls been cut off?"

The sound of the slap echoed through the room. The strength of the slap threw Shariff away from Niazi. The slap came from a man who had maintained his calm all this while – R.K. Rao.

"Don't you dare speak about inhumanity? I will show you now, how to cut the balls out of your bloody dictatorship?" His eyes were absolutely cold.

Rao threw a brown leather bag on the table. "Here are your instructions. Niazi, there is no room for error." He stopped to look at Niazi's face, flooded with tears.

"From this point on, we own every breath you take. You will get your family back unharmed once we are through with the mess you bastards have created." He nodded to confirm to his younger agents that the meeting was over.

Everyone exited, leaving Niazi on his knees and Shariff with a red cheek.

Rao left the dagger in the chest of The Dictator of East Pakistani Armed Force.

Exactly a month later

Shariff was at full attention while sending the telegram. He kept pressing the wooden paddle at regular intervals on the Vibroplex Straight Key device. His pressing of the right paddle generated a series of dashes and squeezing the paddles produced a dit-dah-dit-dah sequence. He had put on a headpiece to mute himself from the other sounds around him except that rhythmic sound. The message read – *'The meet is on 3rd December, be ready.'*

This room had every single element of royalty. A white tiger head mounted on a wall, an oversized wooden wall clock that just recorded quarter past ten, to name a few. Shariff put down the headpiece and got up to stretch his legs. At that moment, the gramophone started playing a classic Hindi song, *'Din dhal jaye haye… raat na jaye'*.

It was Rafi sahib singing about his love life in his mesmerizing voice. The song was so hauntingly beautiful that Niazi found himself remembering his begum with deep sorrow and grief. Shariff walked up to the desk where Niazi was smoking his cigar with his eyes closed and his legs crossed in front, with a huge pile of government documents. Shariff did not want to disturb his master. Niazi broke the silence when he felt Shariff's close presence. Eyes closed he uttered, "I wish I could meet Rafi once…" his voice was shaky and emotional when the song reached its second node.

"Jarur Janab…"

The room had become smoky and the meal on the table was getting cold. As soon as the song ended, the Vibroplex Straight Key beeped with a tick-tack sound. A white paper started printing dots and dashes of an incoming message. Shariff rushed towards it, tore off the printed message and started decrypting the message while decoding the Morse code.

He looked up, and said, "Confirm your identity."

Niazi was in no mood to move an inch; his work was done. He travelled quite regularly to West Pakistan to set the mood of all decision-makers and had just returned for the last time before the big day.

"Jackal," Niazi responded.

Shariff didn't know his code name until now, knowing the trap set by the Indians was on the mark and every high command in Pakistan was inches away from being sucked into it. After all, Niazi was the one who set up that trap, and had successfully gathered unanimous support to order a strike on India. He did follow the exact time frame and instruction provided regularly by R.K. Rao, to create an illusion inside the Pakistani high command that this would be the right time to attack Indians before they could even move an inch.

Shariff typed the code name through dots and dashes again. No reply came and the duo spent the rest of the night listening to other songs of the melody king.

Niazi's better half, Lieutenant-General Hassan Gul, launched pre-emptive air strikes on eleven Indian airbases by the midnight of 3 December 1971. Although apart from Niazi, no one knew that all the air bases were only occupied with huge balloon-shaped dummy Hunter aircrafts. However, the war was defiantly on, leading India's entry into the war of independence for East Pakistan, known as the liberation of Bangladesh. Indian forces were ready since July '71 for this day, the same year, the then Prime Minister Mrs Gandhi and R.K. Rao, chief of RAW were able to seal the arms deal with Israel.

The honourable Prime Minister of India had waited for this day furiously while the number of people killed had reached 2,000,000 civilians. There was genocide in Bangladesh, nearly four hundred thousand women were raped and killed by the Pakistani armed forces, especially Bengali Hindus. Of course these numbers were never true. They did far worse damage than what was out in the news. All this just to prove a point – they would not allow anyone to live with their heads up high, more so the Hindus.

The Pakistanis lasted merely thirteen days in front of the mighty Indian force. It is considered one of the shortest wars in the world's history and was a definite strike on reality for the Pakistani army. Niazi, along with Shariff, spent six more months wondering when they will be freed; they had tried various means to reach the RAW chief. They were turned down each time. They were rotting as POWs, prisoners of war. The political warfare, the aftermath of the Bangladeshi revolution, between India, Pakistan, and foreign peacemakers like Russia and the United Nations took a fair bit of time. Until the Simla Treaty. Later that week, India returned more than 93,000 Pakistani armed forces personnel and civilian intelligence officers, including the 34,000 regular army soldiers, who were POWs.

One day, Niazi was taken away from his POW camp along with his deputy, Shariff Mohammad, and two sentries at the airbase. Shariff Mohammad always had more than a professional relationship with K.A. Niazi and his family. Niazi had led the whole conflict jointly with his Vice-Admiral Shariff Mohammad, Commander of Eastern Naval Command. Shariff always respected him as a mentor in the professional sense and treated him as an elder brother. Shariff was so close to him and his family that he had never left his side when Niazi ruled. And even when he was forced to be a double agent and reduced to nothing. In short, Shariff was the only left descendant of Niazi, who felt and shared his master's pride and pain every step of the way. The man who had immense power and ruled as a dictator was stripped off and his whole kafila had gone astray. Niazi was now no good to Indians as a double agent, and to the Pakistanis as their own military leader.

Inside the Dacca Airbase, an old model aircraft was getting ready to be flown to Pakistan. The aircraft was owned by Pakistani Military and was being refuelled. Niazi and Shariff entered a wooden chamber with glass walls; the sentries were ordered to board the plane with the dictator's belongings. There were quite a lot of bags; after all, he had been the king once.

Niazi found himself in the same equation, surrounded by the same group of men. R.K. Rao with his two deputies and N.K. Osmani, soon to be pronounced as the new military chief of independent Bangladesh.

Niazi spoke first, breaking the deathly silence in the cabin. "I did whatever you asked for. I demand for a fresh identity for all of us. You can do that, right? I won't go back to Pakistan, and I have no use for you now."

Osmani interrupted his premature demands, "Niazi Sahib, how can you presume that you are of no use to us?"

Niazi responded furiously, "*Matlab*?" Niazi's heart pounded as he felt there was more to it.

"Rao Sahib, *ye galat hai*, whatever you are up to. I won't be played again. Where are my wife and child?"

"Niazi, there is a little change of plan. See, we initially thought once you play along with us, we will leave you and your family. But…" Rao spoke with the same posture he was known for.

Hearing the word 'but', Niazi got his furious old gaze back. He grabbed Rao by his collar.

The two deputies fished out their Smith and Wesson revolvers and aimed them at him. Rao signalled not to proceed.

Rao freed himself from Niazi's grip, "See, you still have that monster inside you. We didn't enter this war only to free Bangladesh. Our motto is to correct such an attitude of our neighbour. This bloody attitude cost us billions of innocent lives."

"Niazi, you are a man-eater and you will always be one. Here is your next instruction."

Niazi's head swam in despair, "You can't do this to me. I will not let you do this." He snatched out a gun from Osmani's holster, who was standing near him, but Rao swiftly nabbed it before he could harm anyone or himself.

"Niazi Sahib," Rao slapped him repeatedly on both his cheeks. Niazi had lost his senses, but Rao did manage to bring him back to reality.

"Listen to me now," Rao chewed every word, before instructing further.

"We are returning you last because it will support your reputation as a 'soldier's general'. You are now a scapegoat of your political leaders. You will admit your failures with the Razakar forces, which you raised. Once you are down and outlawed by your own people, you can try some other career options like writing your own biography. It will suit you and could be used as a cover."

"Why? Why are you doing this to me?"

Rao smiled. "To keep my country safe from the likes of you."

Niazi had lost this battle, not only at the war front, but also with his life. He would be free to lead his normal life, but he would remain a POW until his last breath.

"But my family?" he enquired with a broken voice.

"Your wife was sent back to Pakistan; we made her believe that she has lost her daughter in this conflict. Here are some latest snaps of your wife."

Niazi didn't know how to react to this. On one side, Rao had returned his wife back safe as promised, but on the other hand, he had kept his daughter to keep the leash tight enough.

Rao then fixed his eyes on Shariff.

"Shariff Sahib, now it's your turn? How much do you respect this man?"

"I can vouch my life for him."

"I know, yes I know, I am not interested in your life anymore. So it's safe to say you will also be proactive to protect your niece?"

"Yes."

"We are going to keep you as a POW for some more time. From now on, you will be my contact; any message for Niazi will pass through you."

"Now gentlemen, it was a pleasure doing business with you." Rao ended the meeting with a victorious tone.

Niazi was airborne in twenty minutes and Shariff Mohammad was sent to Fort William, Calcutta, India through a different route.

Rao returned to the same cabin.

"Osmani Sahib, did you bring the Angel?"

This was the code name given to this two-year-old baby girl by RAW. The saddest part was that she wasn't in the list of POW issued by RAW. Apart from these men in the wooden cabin, nobody else knew about her existence.

"You really don't trust anyone, do you, Mr Rao?"

The Chief of RAW didn't care to respond to that question and left the room along with the sealed agreement.

From that day onwards, every individual present in this secret meeting proceeded with their life and never met each other. Rao continued achieving his share of success in the field of espionage. Osmani gained immense power in Bangladesh and continued till his last breath. Shariff was transferred from several POW complexes, before finally being released by the Indian government and handed over to the Pakistani government in 1973. Following his return, he began his career in the Navy, despite the fact that the other senior officers were subsequently retired or fired from their services.

Niazi presented a good fight with the Pakistani government to regain his honour, but he knew he was fighting this deceitful battle to lose and to keep his Noori alive. Noori Agah Khan Niazi – the name he had given to his baby girl who would be celebrating her seventh birthday in the winter of '76.

Somewhere in Arunachal Pradesh, Eastern India, 1976

The land of the dawn-lit mountains, it literally embodied that description as the day started with the rising sun. However, it meant a lot more than just a beautiful morning for a seven-year-old girl Noori Khan playing with her dolls in the garden. The local retired military officer Reema Tegi, widow of late Sri Jwala Prasad Tegi, owned this farm with her twenty-two-year-old son Moolchand Tegi, usually called Mannu.

Reema was the assigned guardian to this beautiful, brown-eyed, fair girl. Noori was telling all of her dolls that it was her birthday and they have to be present at the cake cutting ceremony. This farm had a small puppy, barely two months old, who was also part of her invitee list.

Inside the house, Reema heard a loud shriek, followed by the growl of the puppy. She ran towards the garden, thinking that the puppy had probably bit Noori. She found the puppy dead in the garden and Noori holding her rag doll. Reema knew it was Noori's favourite doll. She noticed the dog's fur bitten off at his belly area. When she aggressively turned Noori's face towards her, the sweet Noori had bits of the puppy's fur in her mouth, and her teeth were full of blood. For a second, Reema saw the devil in her. She couldn't believe that Noori had killed the dog for the doll. Noori had never shown any signs of anger before. A switch seemed to have turned on to convert her into this avatar of a devil's child. Noori looked horrified, and she tried to explain herself innocently.

However, Reema was devastated, and being a former military personal, she couldn't let go of her anger towards the girl. She started beating the girl. Meanwhile, Reema kept repeating, "You did it because of the same dirt filled in your blood. It's in your genes!"

Mannu witnessed this beating from the window of his own room from the first floor. Noori was then thrown into a dark room for two days by her Reema aunty. Reema had never tried to let the girl feel that she was her parent. She kept it professional and never felt a fondness for the girl, since she was asked to be the guardian. Reema took very good care of Noori, from her education to a healthy diet. This child was a crucial subject for RAW. That day, what Reema did was out of her code, but she couldn't resist teaching Noori her lesson. Reema never thought Noori's act of violence might need medical attention or psychiatric consultation.

After that horrific day in the farmhouse, nobody ever heard Noori giggling. She always seemed frightened of Reema. Reema, on the other hand, seemed gutted. She had physically abused this child. However, she never reported this to her superiors. Frankly, Reema felt that this girl was never going to be free, as RAW nowadays only cared to send the required money to take good care of this innocent POW. After a few years, in the spring of 1979, out of the blue, a team of men came and took Noori away. Reema never heard of her existence again.

Two

The Red, Contract

Delhi-NCR
August 2012

It was an unusually humid Sunday morning in New Delhi, sucking life out of people. The lone walker to the metro station had a determined walk, a remarkably handsome man with a trim athletic built. The man was in his late twenties and was called Abhimanyu. There was something about his eyes with a piercing gaze, akin to the eyes of a lion.

Abhimanyu was accustomed to Bangalore's pleasant weather where he had been living for the last four years and was a regular employee of a major multinational IT firm. In his circuit, everyone knew him as a spoilt brat with no family name and no known relatives. He was a loner, but a charming one.

The hot and humid climate of New Delhi made him very uncomfortable. His hands were sweaty and a drop of sweat rolled down his chin on to the slot of the fare gates.

There were still two minutes for the next metro to arrive, and there were about ten people waiting to board the train.

Abhimanyu's white shirt was glued to his skin with sweat by the time a metro train arrived and opened its doors, letting everyone in. But he didn't board it. Had he got in, he would have been the only passenger in that car. The automated doors of the metro started to close, but a man rushed past him and boarded the train. The mechanism of the door sensors forced open the doors with a beep. The man was swift and sure-footed.

Abhimanyu didn't see him coming from behind. The man turned towards him and said, "Aren't you coming?"

Abhimanyu then boarded the train and the door slid shut. With a slight jolt, the train left the platform silently. The man was Shubhendu Sarkar, wearing a loose printed shirt and blue jeans along with a blue cap. The Yankee logo was embedded on the front of his cap. They were both meeting after a long time. Shubhendu always looked fitter, smarter and faster than his age, which must be fifty or a couple more.

Shubhendu handed over a sheet of paper to Abhimanyu before speaking.

"Let's sit there!" Shubhendu pointed to the two-seater towards the end of the carriage which connected it to the next one. "Please memorize it and return it."

The slip had an address, handwritten. Abhimanyu memorized it and returned it to him.

The metro reached sector 16 Noida station. Looking at the large number of passengers entering their carriage, Shubhendu suggested, "Let's move out of here. Too many people."

They left their seat and walked up to the next one, then the next one, until they found a carriage which was still quite empty.

Shubhendu started again, while resting his back on the glass handle next to the gate.

"We have fifteen targets, each of whom had a role in the 26/11 blood bath of Mumbai last year."

"Our intel suggested that they have a hierarchy of some sort amongst them. Since January 2012, our different teams have eliminated six of those bastards, but they were lower in the ranks. Every target was pursued by our different teams, investigating and eliminating them as discreetly as possible. You know how it works." He paused for a moment as he saw a boy wearing big headphones approach them.

Shubhendu moved from his place again. This time he went and stood in the middle of the car and Abhimanyu followed him instantly. Two more stops later, Shubhendu spoke again.

"The team which went for the seventh target was making good progress until their team leader requested for reinforcement."

Abhimanyu spoke for the first time since they met, "Why me?" he questioned curiously.

Shubhendu responded tactically. "Why not you?"

"As per the request, it seems like the team leader is somewhat unsettled on the mark, and probably needs a fresh set of eyes before confirming and removing it from the string. We don't make a kill unless and until we are 100% sure. He requested certain skill sets which you have, Rangroot." Shubhendu had a smile on his face, as they both remembered how he used the word Rangroot while training Abhimanyu.

They didn't notice the metro reaching the Yamuna Bank station until passengers swarmed in. The train was instantly overcrowded.

"Any insights, sir?" Abhimanyu whispered.

"I think we should get off at Rajiv Chowk." As Shubhendu spoke, they continued their journey without exchanging words.

Alighting at the desired station, Abhimanyu silently followed Shubhendu to the lower level of the subway to board the yellow line Metro train.

"To answer your question, I am not very sure, but my guess is that with your skills, you're being called to analyse our sources, tap into his activity, and establish a secure network to nail the bastards. Which reminds me of one of our legends in this field – Virat, my partner in crime since our days in DU! Ever since the government scrapped CIT-X and CIT-J divisions in 97, I've lost touch with many of my cronies. I never understood that pissed off, full of madness and ludicrous decision to demolish RAW."

He inhaled deeply and continued. "Anyway, when we all were asked to get back in the game a few years later with a new architecture of RAW, he chose not to be in DIA. Instead, Virat took the road to NTRO division."

He went on, "NTRO is India's elite and a covert technical intelligence gathering agency, a super-feeder agency to all of us, DIA, IB and RAW. They pass on the information about possible suspects or targets to RAW. As soon as the RAW Chief sanctions, NTRO then heads and forms the team, and include members in it such as DIA, IB, also local assets, whomever they want. I have also heard that in this particular mission, they don't even require to have bloody red tapes. The NTRO has always been considered the brain behind RAW, since its formation. These guys are like ghosts; under perfect conditions you won't even see any of our NTRO personnel. But this is different. Our seventh suspect has confused my old pal and that's where you jump in!"

Abhimanyu and Shubhendu got down at the Race Course station.

"Abhimanyu, you may have been known as a wonder boy in your Army days, but remember, it's a totally different ball game to be in the clandestine services. You will be operating in foreign soil, on enemy turf. Don't try to be a hero as you have the bloody knack of doing it. If I were to give you advice, follow your team leader."

Abhimanyu nodded as a schoolboy does to his teacher.

Shubhendu put his hand on his shoulders like a fatherly figure while watching a young woman sitting silently on the farthest steel chairs on that lifeless platform.

"Come back in one piece, will you?"

"Certainly, sir!"

Abhimanyu watched him walk towards the east of the platform, take the emergency exit meant for security personnel only.

On the other side, Shubhendu never understood why he chose those words. You don't patronise your recruit. It makes them vulnerable.

RAW had changed over the years. Everybody knew only what concerned him or her. This structure was like a chain, all the pieces worked together, but the one below didn't know who or what was above their superior. They simply stick to the one above and control the one beneath. It was no more than a puppet for the amusement of the incompetent PMO bureaucracy. However, every now and then when PM's consent was required, the bureaucrats never missed making their presence felt to RAW; the stiffness increasing since 26/11. The media trail of RAW incompetence was negligible to the harassment they receive from the PMOs. The decision makers in the PMO had made that embarrassing moment of 26/11 as an amusement of government and politicos. Then came the day when a stronger opposition, critical approach pushed the PMO to take the matter with utter sincerity and gave RAW a go-ahead with full authority. This led them to get the removal process started, which meant wiping off the leeches, aka terrorists.

Abhimanyu took an auto rickshaw to the address he had memorized. IGI Delhi Airport, his new quarters for the night. At the international airport, he reported at the Air India counter where he was aided to a temporary room inside the airport. The room was like a small bunker for security personnel, not spacious enough, but comfortable for a soul with basic logistics. There was nothing else to do, so he waited. Just when his eyes were heavy with sleep, someone slipped an envelope into the bunker and left hurriedly. The envelope had tickets to Izmir and his new credentials. His cover was that of an IT employee travelling on business VISA to set up a new Data Centre in Izmir, Turkey, for Ubsoft group. He was to be the strategic operations analyst, was married but widowed. Why the fuck widowed? He chuckled at himself! The envelope also had a file with the instruction 'TO BE BURNT AFTER USE' written across in red.

Next day 2.30 p.m.
Izmir Airport

After the immigration check, Abhimanyu took the passage to the counter for Euro Car, a car rental service inside the airport.

"Hello, there should be a car booked in my name Arya, here's the receipt."

Abhimanyu was now Arya – Arya Pratap Singh.

This ancient port city had been subject to the influence of multiple cultures from the early Neolithic ages. From its first look it seemed like the city was struggling to let go of its multicultural heritage, but modern development was taking a toll anyway. The buildings influenced by Roman architecture were steadily paving way for the glassed skyscrapers.

HalilRifat Pasha Mansion, Izmir, Turkey
8 p.m.

The old yet magnificent HalilRifat Mansion stood proud, defying every attempt of man and nature to bring it down. Once home to a grand Vizier of the Ottoman Empire, it was now transformed into an Education Centre and Library.

A staircase on the left of this mansion led down to the neighbourhoods of Izmir. The road down the stairs was made of bricks, probably by the ones that came off the mansion when it was partially burnt down. Arya stood facing the Rifat Mansion with seven wooden windows, and behind him there was a door which led to another mansion.

Arya kept glancing back and forth from the windows to the doors for a possible sign from his contact, but so far there was nothing. He realized that nothing would happen before 8:12

p.m. As per the instructions in that envelope, at precisely this time he took out his brand of cigarette pack so that the name on it could be seen by anybody who was watching him. He took out a cigarette and dropped it. He cursed himself aloud and at the same time counted till ten and lit another one. That's precisely when a woman arrived from behind him. It was as if she came out of thin air. An absolute treat to the eyes. She had curly, dusky brown hair managed by a scarf. The little mole on her upper lip towards the left was a killer, but it was the eyes. This stunning beauty had eyes so beautiful, anyone could fall for her just by looking at her eyes. To his utmost surprise, she turned out to be a hooker.

She offered her services for 500 lira. Arya was trying to brush her away, but it seemed like the girl had taken a liking to him.

Arya had had enough. He was about to charge at the woman, when she giggled and said, "Didn't know RAW had started recruiting impotent men."

It took him a few moments to realize that the girl *was* the contact.

"Now don't stand there like a gaping pig! Get along."

When the drunk couple coming from the other side had crossed them and reached a considerable distance, this woman opened the back door. He followed her to a long, narrow room, which was so dim Arya could hardly see a thing. A doorway opened onto a set of wooden stairs in desperate need of repair. The odour of urine and faeces was strong; she opened the adjacent door. This was the entrance of a pub of some sort, through the pantry area. As they got out of the pantry, Arya could hear the Jazz music more clearly. This place was really a *meyhane* – rough Turkish bar. Uneven windows, cold floor with spilled drinks, and a low ceiling. The place was dense with thick smoke, and it stank of sweat and cheap tobacco. He noticed a group of seven men sharing kebabs and drinks. These looked like workers straight out of a construction site. On the other side was a couple – the woman looked like a prostitute sitting on her customer's thighs. At that moment while scanning the place, he saw a man sitting right at the end of the bar. They made eye contact and the man signed him with his two fingers. As Arya started towards him, the bartender offered him

"Scotch whisky? Cognac?"

"Rum, if you have."

He served him Old Monk.

Arya walked towards the shady figure sitting in the darkest corner of the pub, of course, the boss. The spymaster who ran this team, and most likely many others. From now on, Arya would answer only to him. Until he was proven dead. He was regarded in all major departments of RAW, NTRO, NSA and his own department, DIA. The man was dressed tediously, and was approaching his late-forties. His shiny black leather jacket showed the body of a sprinter. He smelled of a spirit, and was smoking a cigarette. He gave a hacking cough when Arya sat next to him.

Arya noticed his contact, the girl, sitting with the bartender and the cook. The bartender served them drinks, while they chatted in a low pitch. How he wished he could hear what she was saying!

"What do think of him?" She had a scrutinizing glare.

The bartender passed his judgment.

"You know what they say, girl?" The cook and the girl looked at him for a possible witty answer which he was known for.

"Never trust a guy who likes rum! Nope... never!"

Then the bartender went back to clearing his *meyhane*, and suddenly shouted at those seven workers and then at the prostitute in local Turkish language. He harshly made a gesture with his hand and demanded them to leave the bar since it was time for him to close for the day. They were not happy; it was barely half past nine. However, they knew him as they were his regulars, so they left the pub in ten minutes. It was then that Arya realized that the final member of the squad was actually the client of that prostitute, who joined the huddle along with the young woman, cook and the barman.

"Any problem finding us here?" the boss spoke.

"No sir. Except that the girl over there did take me for a ride." Arya sensed that Virat only asked out of courtesy, so he ended the matter. They sat silently for another few rounds of Jack Daniels and Old Monk. The watch recorded a quarter past twelve when Virat spoke again.

"Let's go for a walk, Arya. The rest of you stay here. I'll show him around and be back in an hour or so. Come on!"

"Our target is Jan Mohammad Baloch a.k.a 'Mir'. He is a Syrian diplomat residing in Izmir, Turkey. We call him 'The money man'. Contrary to his shabby looks, he is very smart and equally ruthless. He doesn't leave any trace behind him, travels heavily guarded and lives a low life. He neither drinks nor likes prostitutes, so you know it is not easy to penetrate his personal front," Virat concluded the introduction.

"We have learnt that his roots are connected to Kashmir; you will be surprised to know that he is of Indian origin. Mir was born in the small village of Badgam district in Jammu and Kashmir in the 70s, the part administered by India. We believed he completed his graduation from Srinagar's Sri Pratap College. His half-brother, Ahmedullah, was a leader of one faction of a militant wing, who organized militancy in Kashmir in 1989, along with some more radicals like him. All of these people were Mir's godfathers. Soon after the Indian military action, he was sent away, probably to Syria. We have no knowledge about his whereabouts from 1990 to '98, but he popped into our radar as a Syrian in 99 as a prominent Syrian diplomat. Rest you can read whenever you have time. Let's sit there..." Virat pointed to the lone bench fixed alongside the street, while handing over an encrypted phone.

The cold breeze blew strongly and the street light flickered. Arya toggled through the encrypted phone and Virat admired houses on the opposite side of the boulevard.

Arya noticed Tanveer, the prostitute lover, was a Turkish intelligence officer, locally known as MIT.

"It beats me! Why are the Turks helping us?" he questioned Virat.

"It's been three years since I met him; he is a good guy. Likely, the only fault he made was murdering his mistress out of rage. Same old story – has a kid and a wife. So I helped him clear his mess. Since then he has helped us. Now don't ask, whether he actually killed his mistress," he chuckled, for the first time.

"As far as MIT knows, we are here because of some Iraqi angle and Tanveer is managing the Turks well. He is the one who provides us all the extra intel about Mir's schedules and whereabouts."

Virat sniffed and coughed hard, shivering under the jacket.

"Well, I am done for the day." He stood up with his hands in the jacket pockets.

"You know your way back right?"

"Yes…" Arya nodded.

Virat left him at the cold night post and disappeared in the darker portion of the alley near the end of that beautiful boulevard. Arya went back to that phone, reading more about the team members. The girl's name was documented as Zehana Ayberk. She was in her mid-twenties. In the picture, her hair was rich raven black with tawny shades which she owed to an Indian father and a Turkish mother. She scored well in her field test and was an expert data analyst. If at all a honey trap was needed, there couldn't be anyone more perfect than her. Honey traps had always been an old protocol used by most of the teams all around the intelligence community.

The cook Ramanna, was a tech wizard and was from the Cyber Ops division of NTRO. He held a degree in engineering from MIT, Massachusetts with a scholarship but the entire NTRO staff knew that he had cracked into the MIT server and declared himself as a scholar of the batch. He was passionate about cooking and had a vivid sense of humour when it came to technology. He was in the core design team which maintained RAW's encryption.

Farooq, the canny bartender, was a sleeper agent. Primarily used as a safe housekeeper here in Turkey, he was ex-Indian Military. He had been an asset in his prime – the sole reason why his superiors had thought it best for him to be a sleeper agent for as long as he wished. Nevertheless, he was always top notch then, and still had gutsy foresights. He prepared the escape route single-handedly. This man knew how to clean up his tracks.

The team looked efficient enough to crack the mission, but as per primary findings, this team were sitting ducks. Arya wanted to read more, but was interrupted by his own yawn of tiredness. A car passed by him and its beam made that silver name plate glow for a second, which hung in front of that lavishing villa.

'*Atatürk Caddesi No 9/B, Yalýkavak, Bodrum*'

Something snapped inside him.

He knew that address. He'd seen it somewhere before. Seen it or read it? Where? His mind raced and those tired eyes grew wider. Shit! It's where Mir lived. It was his bloody house!

He promptly stood up and vacated the bench near the flickering street light. His mind raced with a vivid sense of imagination, as if Virat was living on the edge. He probably had a habit of watching his targets up close like this, maybe every night. This was a wrong approach; he was breaking protocol. Did RAW make a mistake choosing him as a team leader? He thought about this while making sure nobody followed him on his way back.

Three

The Red, Glimpse

Three days had passed by since Arya had arrived. They were tracking Mir's every movement and trying to figure out their way to sneak into his territory and set up surveillance on him. So far they had only managed to capture some audio frequency from an open coffee shop, where Mir paid a visit every day sharp at 9 a.m. with his security. He came here often, occasionally to meet different people and talk about politics. Setting up surveillance required a great deal of planning and labour. Zehana and Ramanna were getting efficient at this. They had been doing this for the last three months – holding high-frequency mikes, frequently changing their positions accordingly, and most importantly, improvising as and when needed. Just by looking at the extent of Mir's security staff, it was evident that both Zehana and Ramanna were doing an excellent job, or that Mir knew about them and he couldn't care less.

It was Arya's fourth day at work and Tanveer joined him in his car. They chatted as they waited for Mir to leave his house.

It was Arya's turn to tail first and Virat would catch up later. Merely a minute had gone by when Mir's car left the driveway and pulled out on 1416 SK, heading towards the Murselpasa Blv Street, the usual route for a sip of coffee. It was a bit early by usual standards. Arya cranked up his car, but it failed to start. He tried again, but this time his Ford Taunus '89 coughed and then suddenly died again.

"People, what's your status?" Virat's voice came over the earpiece.

"Virat, the Ford is not starting!" Tanveer responded to the message as he ran towards his car to pursue Mir. They knew where Mir was headed, so Tanveer would catch up with him soon, thought Arya.

"He has changed his route. I repeat. Mir has deviated from his usual course to Gazi Blv, and he is definitely in a rush!" Tanveer screamed while starting his car as he kept his sight fixed on the boulevard.

Virat came rushing with his Citroen C-Elysée and stopped dead ahead of Arya.

"Get it fixed!" he said with clenched teeth before rushing to join Tanveer in the pursuit of the Prix Peugeot 301. Arya tried his luck again, but the old car was in no mood for a spin. Zehana and Farooq were on night patrol and resting with Ramanna, who was down with a sore stomach. However, he was monitoring the surveillance feeds by hacking into traffic cameras. No one would have thought that bastard would choose this fateful day to change his bloody course.

In another two minutes, Arya got the news that Tanveer had caught up with Mir and had him in sight. As he continued to tail him, Virat joined him as well. Arya came out of the car, lit his cigarette and in frustration gave the tyres a kick.

We could have lost Mir today, thought Arya. He felt guilty for not checking the car. He finished his cigarette when he overheard Ramanna saying with a sigh, "Here... she comes!"

A handsomely dressed woman in her early forties comes out from the house. She was dressed in a grey Chesterfield coat over a linen pantsuit with crocodile heeled sandals. She looked elegant and had her face covered with black sunglasses. With her was a black Labrador retriever on a retractable leash.

"Aisha Bahar! Do not worry, mate! We have already checked her out."

"What do you mean by checking her out?" asked Arya.

"Every now and then, she takes her Labrador for a walk," Ramanna concluded.

"I am not concerned about what she does or doesn't. What I am concerned here is have you ever seen a woman all dressed up in formal wear talking a dog out for poo?" Arya snapped with irritation.

"No," came the reply.

"I am following her." Arya had read about her in Mir's profile.

"But what happens if Virat needs you?" asked Rammanna.

"Send Zehana and keep an eye on the house, will you?" Arya suggested.

Virat's voice crackled over the centralized connected earpieces. Mir's car was two cars ahead of them.

"I don't think he's trying to lose me – it's just that he's a fast driver. He's switching lanes back and forth."

Arya tailed the woman and the dog. When the two came to the Esplanade in Kordon area, she loosened the leash on the dog; it bounded over a low hedge and onto the small tree. After a couple minutes, she tugged the leash and the dog jumped back across the hedge, as they continued down the street.

"Who walks her dog in a cream linen pantsuit at nine in the morning?" Tanveer questioned, referring Arya to Virat.

"Yes, Tanveer, that's my point," Arya confirmed confidently as he wanted to pursue his hunch.

"Or maybe she is just a bored, crazy lady wanting to get out of the house!" Virat replied with sarcasm.

Virat was understandably not happy about Arya following his intuition. But he didn't object.

Arya meanwhile crossed the street and took a sidewalk right opposite to Aisha. The pursuit on foot reached a nearby street market. The shops were open and filled with people. The street vendors crowding onto the street made the street extremely narrow, forcing people to walk in a single file. While following her further, Arya noticed a big bald, muscular man, possibly a Turkish. He had his head down and was peeping frequently at him, ten feet ahead of Aisha. A glare exchanged between them, and then suddenly a hawker blocked Arya's sight. When the hawker had passed, the bald man was nowhere in sight. It's a unique phenomenon of one spy crossing path with another in this part of the world. You could tell them just by the way they all dress up – shoes, jacket, sunglasses and their steady stance.

Are some other agencies also keeping a watch on Mir and Aisha? Possibly yes! Or am I being watched by security services hired by Mir himself?

This thought distracted him for a couple of minutes and he lost Aisha. He paced himself scanning every shop randomly.

After a few blocks, that busy old street market turned into a rather urban marketplace – fashionable and less crowded and a series of designer shops like Gucci, Giorgio Armani changed the whole scene. Suddenly he spotted the retriever. The bitch was with a security guard in front of the ZARA showroom.

"She must be in there!" He heaved a sigh of relief. He waited for another ten minutes for her to come out, but there was no sign of her.

I need to keep her in sight, he thought again. He was restless and needed to confirm that she was actually inside. So he crossed the road and entered the ZARA showroom. The bitch sniffed him when he crossed her. The shop was not so big, so he took a few seconds to realize that she was not in there. Maybe she had sneaked out through the back door. He took a T-shirt from the men's collection and went towards the fitting rooms. Arya started pushing the doors one by one. As he was about to push the third door, it opened and Aisha Bahar emerged up close, for him to get a whiff of her peach scented perfume.

She definitely looked younger for a woman in her forties. She had a straight nose with high cheekbones. She was wearing a rosy lip colour highlighted with a darker red around the corners of her full lips. This accentuated her glowing peaches and cream skin tone. She had a high forehead and straight hair neatly tied up. Her eyes were ocean blue, with artificial eyelashes. Her beauty had an unreal quality, like the ones viewed in the cinema. She was trying out a red feathery gown. It revealed her shoulders and the neckline plunged down to expose her cleavage.

"Do you mind?" she demanded of him blocking her way. Arya was completely dazed. He moved aside.

"Thank you," and she went forth.

He took the next door and stayed there pretending to try on the new T-shirt. Meanwhile he got information from Virat and Tanveer that Mir had stopped in the Port of Izmir and had gone inside the container storage yard, which was further confirmed by Ramanna that he might be on his way to container no 367898712D, which he owned. Virat and Tanveer were hot in pursuit.

Arya overheard Aisha's soft sophisticated voice. She liked the dress very much and now she wanted it to be adjusted and tailored. Arya gathered himself together, and left the showroom. He bought a scarf from a street vendor to keep his cover. She was back on the same street after fifteen minutes and started walking ahead. After a twenty minute walk further ahead, she stopped in front of a small departmental store called TESCO, which sold household items. Chaining her dog to the sidewalk barrier, she entered the store. He couldn't enter this time at the risk of blowing his cover. If she noticed him again, she might get suspicious of him being a stalker. He watched her from the other side of the road, through the glass walls of the store. His hunch of Aisha being involved in Mir's dirty business was weakening by the minute.

She went to the last row.

"Dammit! Why was this dog getting so agitated?" Arya was getting annoyed at her dog which was barking furiously.

She was doing all she could to unleash herself from the chain

Oh no! The bitch was barking at him! This would blow his cover for sure; he instantly turned around facing the shop named Pet Afrika. He noticed this store was a showroom selling dog food along with pet accessories. His thoughts travelled to Aisha. Was she here to buy cheap dog food? He turned back in a flash and saw she was on her way back, carrying a small pack of Pedigree's dog food and now a very calm bitch on the leash.

'Women like her, so conscious of their looks and apparel, don't shop for the price. Why did she choose the departmental store over this showroom across the street? There is something wrong here,' he thought, as he ran back into the store in a flash and went to the same aisle where he last saw her. That aisle had piles of Pedigree and other brands of dog food. His hunch was now proving to be correct, as he overheard again on the earpiece that Virat and Tanveer found Mir doing nothing interesting at the Dock. He had just gone inside to check if the container was ready to be delivered on the same day. He could have done that over the phone itself.

Arya stopped at a point, as something caught his eyes between the Pedigree packets. It was a bottle!

It was a bottle of coffee powder placed in between two packets of dog food. The bottle looked properly sealed. Was it left here by mistake or purposely? He started scratching his head and then realized his fingers were sticky. On examining it, he found it to be some kind of glue stuck to the bottle's price tag. On rubbing a little, the price tag came off and underneath he found stuck a small black object, the size of a mole.

It was a microdot use to store data. He placed the microdot in his cell phone's memory chip cabinet and Ramanna cloned its data remotely. He placed the price tag back along with the microdot and put it back on the shelf exactly where he had found it. His work was half done here. If Mir had tried to pass on the information to someone through Aisha, Arya could expect someone to pay a visit here very soon. He came out of the store and lit his second smoke for the day. He waited for Virat and Tanveer to pick him. He thought about Aisha, a queen, by all means. She had an air around her and maintained a completely normal demeanour during the whole time. It seemed like an everyday affair for her.

During the course of his life as a spy, Arya knew one thing. Sometimes, you had to defy protocol to follow a hunch and get a breakthrough. It was the nature of the job. Thanks to his Ford breaking down, otherwise they would not have tracked Aisha and reached here. Mir cleverly passed information right under their noses, using other means.

At the base

Ramanna started with a sigh. "Yes, it has fifteen names, an offshore account number and a map of some sort of a building."

"That's it?" asked Arya.

"Yes."

"Fifteen names that aren't found in our database. What interested me the most was the location of this offshore account. It's in Bangladesh in the name of one Sameer Qureshi. When I went to check the transactions of this account, I found Sameer is just an alias," Ramanna rattled off.

"The offshore account holder's name is Farahat Husain. This Bangladeshi banker's name has appeared in our database. We have had this guy on our radar for a long time, a forger of fake IDs and basically a human trafficker."

"Any latest transaction on this account?" Virat enquired.

"Yes, a week ago, over two million USD has been deposited. Not a wire transfer so I can't track who did it," replied Ramanna.

"I can't believe all we have got is a bloody forger," Virat sighed with frustration. Ramanna had a cranky smile on his face.

"Virat, the real intel is not what's in the dot, it's the dot itself. Every microdot has a blank space referred to as a signature chunk in our world, so I broke the chunk and found a digital mark of its creator named as Marcos. I found his IP address too, which is still active and is in a place called Alacati, the old town in Izmir."

Ramanna had a smug smile on his face while he played with his pen.

Four

The Red, Shadow

Monday, 12 September
10 p.m.

It had started raining along with flashes of lightning.

"You awake?" Arya enquired.

"Hardly. You want a nap, go ahead."

"No thanks. Maybe later."

At 10:30 p.m.

"By the way," Arya asked again, "Is the weather always like this over here?"

"Atchoo! No, this fucking weather makes me feel terrible."

12 a.m.

Faint music played somewhere down the road, while the soundless city lay behind them. The sound of the music was hypnotic and Arya fought hard to stay awake. He took a cigarette from the flat box in his pocket, and went outside the car to light it up.

35

1:15 a.m.

"Wake up, Arya," said Zehana.

"Hmmm…"

"I think we are in trouble here. A night patrol car is coming our way. If they suspect us, then our cover is at risk!" observed Zehana.

"Act drunk, and when I give a signal, drink this!" Arya handed over a small bottle with a transparent liquid to Zehana.

"What is this?" enquired Zehana

"Nothing, just do as I say."

Arya poured whiskey on himself and Zehana.

A police car stopped right in front of them, its headlight on their faces.

"What are you doing here, sir?" asked the officer in Turkish.

"What? No Turkish, talk only English!"

"I said what are you doing out here in the middle of the night, sir? Have you been drinking and driving?" he asked again.

"I am not drunk,"Arya responded.

"Could you please step out of the car, sir?" insisted the officer.

"Okay, okay. I am coming out." Arya gave a signal to Zehana and stepped out.

The moment she drank the liquid, Zehana started feeling uncomfortable and vomited. In a flash, she was out of the car, vomiting.

"I think she is pregnant, but not drunk!"

Arya also acted as if he was going to throw up.

The police officers gave a disgusted look, pushed Arya towards his car and walked away.

"Just a bunch of drunken jerks," the officer muttered in Turkish to his fellow officer and they drove away.

Arya stayed on the bonnet of the car facing the warehouse and noticed a person coming out and walking towards them.

Arya then passed a water bottle to Zehana and helped her get back inside the car.

"I am not going to drink anything from you anymore, Arya!" Zehana replied and gave him a dirty look.

"Don't worry you will be fine in two minutes. Keep monitoring the warehouse. I am going to follow the man who just came out of the warehouse. He seems to be the same guy who was watching me when I was trailing Aisha today morning," he whispered while helping her get back to her seat.

The big muscular man wore a raincoat and carried a briefcase. He had a hard, bony face beneath a hat. As he approached them, Arya bent down towards Zehana and kissed her on her lips. Zehana's eyes dilated and she started breathing heavily. It was a very awkward moment for both of them, but he had no other way to take cover. After a few seconds, when Arya stopped to get some breath, he found the man standing five feet away, lighting a cigarette.

Arya had to carry on with the kiss and Zehana was fully prepared this time. In his mind, Arya was hoping Zehana would understand this situation and not slap him afterwards. Zehana meanwhile happened to pull the lever on the seat and this completely reclined the seat. Zehana found Arya on top of her completely. However, this was a deliberate move to get hold of the Walther PPK Pistol from the pistol holder from inside Zehana's coat. Arya could feel her whole body tighten and get into the act by holding Arya's face

Abhishek Srivastava

and kissing his neck. This act was blowing out of proportion. With the outside temperature dropping a few notches, the warmth in the car seemed to engulf them. They became bolder and as their faces came closer, their breath intermingling, Arya and Zehana forgot the world around them momentarily. The moment passed away too soon, a single eye contact between them and something snapped! Arya looked up to see the bald guy stride past their car. The bald guy was certain that they were a drunken couple enjoying their night out. Arya dragged himself out of the car and tossed the pistol back to Zehana. He reached out for his gun Beretta 8045 cougar .45 from beneath his jacket and checked to see if it was still loaded. He was trying to calm his mind from the wanton act he was just involved in! They looked at each other awkwardly. Arya just managed to say 'sorry'.

"Change of plan. Give me thirty seconds, Zehana," said Arya. "Then follow along slowly. Keep your distance and switch off your headlights. Meanwhile, inform Virat and ask him to cover both the exits for a while."

After walking ten steps ahead, Arya heard footsteps hurrying away from him towards the east side of the warehouse, towards the city. To the west lay the railway station. Arya walked quickly to the east side of the warehouse, paused at the corner and had a quick look at it. Nobody was there. Where the hell did he go? There was only one street he could have taken from there, thought Arya. Moving swiftly, he reached the street, turned the corner and there he was – at least somebody was. Then the man glanced over his shoulders and turned right, down a narrow alley. He had most likely spotted Arya, but so what? Just a man, plodding along, on a miserable night.

Arya walked past the alley until he reached the far corner and moved out of sight. He saw a loading dock across from him and moved towards it quickly. Dropping one foot in a pothole on a rocky stretch, he hurried up the steps and stood in the corner of the shuttered entryway and the wall. *Had the watch and wait for game begun yet?* Arya silently thanked his mentor Shubhendu Sarkar for his first lesson – Don't enter a place until you have located the exit points. If things get nasty, your best guide would always be the 1,400-gram brain sitting on the top of your body.

A few seconds later, the Peugeot turned the corner behind him and Arya signalled to Zehana to stay where she was.

Arya looked at his watch, it showed '2.45 a.m.' The intensity of the rain had increased, so had the cold.

It was 3.00 a.m. What was the bald man doing down there? Was there a way out to another street? He was getting restless. Should I go out and investigate? Arya felt agitated. He approached the alley, which was as dead as the night.

Baldy had disappeared, but where? Arya jogged along the sheer wall with every muscle tensed and ready for any action. Then he appeared in front of a doorway, just at the foot of the alleyway. A door that came out of nowhere, would lead into another warehouse, for sure. The door was meant to be invisible during daytime as the texture was a bit off and it had almost the same colour as the sheer wall.

Arya freed the Beretta's clip, checked it and clicked it back into place. Then he placed himself on one corner, bent his right knee to the ground and pointed the gun towards the door. All the time making sure of his balance. A shot with your name on it was always a possibility. Therefore, if someone really had that intention, he might shoot a bullet aiming right at your chest or head.

However, in this position, there is always a 70 percent – 30 percent chance that your enemy will miss the first shot and you can take him by surprise. Arya turned the knob and pushed the door open. No bullets fired at him. A narrow passage opened out to a large square room that looked like a small office. The room was flat and empty, except for a tanned leather sofa. Arya saw a staircase leading to the second floor on the right. He could see the second floor as well. It looked like a small library from his end. The air was thick with a pungent smell of weed. He rolled over and then dived to two feet ahead, looking behind the sofa. Silence greeted him as his eyes adjusted to the darkness around him. He got up and moved forward to climb the stairs, but he knew it was hopeless. The bald man was long gone.

Suddenly something moved or someone shifted. The sound of weight shifting on board, came from somewhere above him. He waited, shifted the gun to his other hand and wiped his sweaty palms on his trousers. He felt his throat and lips go dry, so he gulped and rolled his tongue around his lips to make them wet. Again, he heard the sound almost directly above his head. So, there is a third floor? How did one go up there? There was no floor above him. He discovered a passage ahead of him with books stacked on both sides. He saw a rope dangling from the roof with a knot on at one end. It wasn't a stairway, but a foldable wooden ramp. There was a sound of running feet above.

Arya scurried up the ramp and dived flat at the top, his head landed just below the roof level. He got up quickly to get a better look, but even with the light from the first floor, darkness enveloped the top floor. The roof was low and couldn't accommodate his 5"11' height. So he ducked his head while pointing the Beretta ahead. He sniffed and then shouted out in Turkish. "Come out from where you're hiding, and let me see your hands!"

Nothing happened and suddenly his gaze fell on a piece of cloth kept behind the five feet wooden selves. It looked familiar.

"Don't shoot me, please, please, please. I beg you for my life!"

A loud cry was heard. He managed to locate the voice and saw a woman, still pointing his gun and a lighter towards her. She was sitting with her legs folded to her chest, her head down. Her hands were clasped together, her fingers intertwined, her face hidden behind her hair.

"Who are you?" Arya inquired.

The answer was somewhat unexpected and the devastated face was unrecognizable until he heard her voice.

She identified herself as Aisha Bahar in a shaky voice. She lifted her face as she spoke. Her face, then he saw it, the sight of which shook him from head to toe. It was full of fresh scars, but the blood had dried and caked her hair to her face. She was having trouble speaking since her lips were swollen at the corners and her nose was bleeding. They were torn and he saw dried blood on her legs from her waist downwards. It looked like she had been raped and then beaten. Beaten so hard, Arya could see her damaged collarbone. She tried to express herself, sensing he had come to help her. He promised to rescue her and was stunned for a minute. Exactly at that moment, he sensed someone was behind him; it was a moment too late. A hard blow on the left side of his head left Arya senseless. All he managed to see before collapsing on the wooden floor was the smiling face of the bald guy.

◆

As Arya slowly returned to his senses, after almost twenty minutes, he was hauled by foot into a very masculine chamber that smelled of Moroccan pipe tobacco or *shisha*.

"Hello Mr Arya, I hope we are not being a pain in your ass."

"Well, let me tell you my feelings. Switch off the lights and let me see your face, asshole."

He made a sound of clicking his fingers and the lights were switched off. After a moment, Arya's vision adjusted and he could see a man with a bony face, beard, and moustache, wearing a yellow shirt and a pair of white pants in front of him. He immediately recognized the man as Jan Mohammad Baloch, aka 'Mir' – his target, now his captor.

◆

"What? What did he just say?" Mir asked his three companions whether someone had heard Arya's last words. Arya had bid his farewell to Zehana. He could not do much to save her, could he!

"He is not going to talk, Boss, not until he feels the pain himself. I told you before, you unnecessarily killed my bitch, such a waste!" said Bulla 'The Butcher'.

"Do what you want to do with him, but remember, he shouldn't die."

"I want him alive when I come back from Budapest. You have three days, break him!" replied Mir and left the room, wiping the blood from his handgun, leaving without a hint of remorse at killing Zehana.

"Now things will get interesting for you, Mr Arya," sneered Bulla and started beating him on the shoulder with a rod.

"This is just a warm-up, so that you do not resist us later."

It took two days for a man like Bulla 'The Butcher' to see that his enhanced interrogation techniques were not working on Arya. Surely he cried, even bled and coughed on occasions, but never pleaded for mercy. This made Bulla a little uncomfortable. He had tried it all – prying out nails, suffocating him with a wet towel, and pouring gallons of water over him. Nothing worked.

It was then that Bulla decided to take this interrogation to the next level.

"Strip him and hang him with his hands tied!" Bulla shouted out his order to his minions. Bulla then drenched Arya from top to bottom with water. His two companions brought out the defibrillator, stuck two patches on Arya's chest, and slid a wooden stick between his teeth.

Arya was hanging as a dead body, eyes open; he was breathing but did not have the energy or desire to resist. The room smelled acidic first and then the metallic odour of blood seeped in.

"Bulla, he won't survive it. Look at him, he is dead meat. His pulse is bleak."

However, this didn't affect The Butcher's determined hands, as he tested the flow of current by joining the two nodes of wire which caused an immediate spark. That spark can force any human soul to beg for his life, but here, there was no expression from Arya.

"Hello! Do you know what we are going to do with you? I have seen people pee in their pants even before the shock, and after that, they shit in their...."

Nevertheless, Bulla didn't wait for Arya's response and put the two nodes of wire on his manhood. His whole body shook until Bulla removed those nodes. The shock was so intense that Arya broke the piece of wood placed in between his jaws. The lights also dimmed for a few seconds in the room. This was followed by a beeping sound from the defibrillator, which then changed to single beep after every interval.

Beep... Beep... Beep... Beeeeeeeeeeeeeeeeeeeeeeep

One of them shouted, "Shit, he is losing his pulse!"

All three of them looked at the screen of the defibrillator. The pulse wave was going down and down and down and then finally became a straight line. The other one cut Arya's hand loose, Arya's body had no life left, so he just fell on the man.

"I told you, man, don't do it. Mir is going to kill us all!" One of them started pounding Arya's chest to bring him back to life.

For the first time, Bulla's voice was shaking and he hardly managed to say, "Adrenaline... pass me that adrenaline, you fucker!" to the third minion still standing near the defibrillator.

Five

The Red, Angel and Demon

London, 1979

Shariff was happy to be able to get her niece back from RAW's custody. However, Shariff thought it be best to keep Noori's existence a secret – her mother having died a year before Noori's release and father struggling to get his honour back. There was no future left for the child in Pakistan, except hatred, hardship and misfortune.

It was almost ten by the time they finished their dinner. Shariff was in his study, in the posh hotel room, reading some important papers related to the Pakistani government's new policies, when he felt someone enter the room. He realized that Noori had entered the room stark naked. Completely bewildered, he left his table to go near her. Without saying a word, Noori reached out to unzip his pants. Shocked to his core, he stopped her to enquire in a shaky voice, "*Ye... kya kar rahee hai aap Noori?*"

To his utter surprise, Noori replied, "Did I do something wrong, uncle? Please don't throw me into the dark room. I get scared."

45

He gently took her back to her room and got her dressed. Shariff then ordered lots of ice-cream for her. And after a while, when she was relaxed enough, he enquired her about her actions. Noori responded that back in the farmhouse, "Mannu uncle always kept me safe from Reema aunty. In return, Mannu uncle used to ask me to unzip his pants and then…"

Shariff heard the horrifying tale while tears rolled down his cheeks.

The next day, a friend who happened to be a doctor confirmed that it was a case of child molestation. There were signs of the forceful act of violence and abuse and she had been involved in sexual intercourse. When the doctor asked about the identity of Noori and her history, Shariff declined to disclose it.

Autumn of 1981

Two years after that incident, Shariff was on his way from Seoul international airport to an unknown location in the heart of the Korean capital. He had two photographs in his hand. On the left was the picture of Noori when she was ten years and on the right was the picture of Noori at the age of twelve. There were huge differences between the photographs. Noori at twelve had a defined cheekbone, lips like petals and extremely straight hair; they were the result of a reconstruction surgery done to her face.

Seoul was covered in red and yellow leaves, an autumnal feature in Korea. Apart from the beauty of this unfamiliar city, Shariff was also admiring Noori's new face and how successful the surgery had been. The doctors struggled initially to avail the latest technologies but Shariff used Niazi's and his own hidden fortunes to provide the Korean clinic with all the equipment and the best surgeons from London. At the clinic, he met the new Noori. She wasn't looking all that gorgeous as in the picture. Large braces, made of brass and steel, were screwed onto her face. It looked painful. There was clutched onto her jaws to lift up her cheekbones and other required reconstruction. Her skeletal figure confirmed that she had to be on a liquid diet for this surgery. They had a very nice chat in the garden of the clinic and Noori later complained to Shariff that the food was tasteless and she was dying to have ice cream. Shariff quickly dismissed her and explained that she couldn't risk having any such food items till the final stages of the surgery were over. This poor kid was growing without a single man or a woman who cared for her desires.

Noori at her age had had the most horrible childhood – full of misery and loneliness.

5 years later, 1986

It's been five years since Noori became Anaya McQuillen. Anaya McQuillen, a British national who had a British mother and father of Kashmiri descent. Anaya's father grew up in Seoul and had a job in a chemical plant in Seoul. Her mother was from Lincoln city, a county town of Lincolnshire, England. It was recorded that Anaya's mother died under suspicious circumstances after being admitted to a facility for tackling her depression, right after Anaya's birth. A large sum of money and a pile of forged documents provided the perfect moment for Noori to disappear and reappear as Anaya McQuillen.

Shariff was greatly disturbed by the last conversation he had on the phone with Anaya's combat trainer. After her reconstruction surgery, she was doing strict combat training in a different location. Her trainer confirmed to Shariff that Anaya was too soft to become a human weapon. She failed in all the departments constantly for a year or so. When Shariff heard that statement, he erupted in fury and stated, "I am not spending a million dollars just to hear how incompetent you all have been. I will be there in a week and I better be impressed," he concluded.

Shariff had to arrange to make that unscheduled stop at Seoul; he took the liberty since he was due to retire from his naval career in a few months. On arrival, he had a heated discussion with the entire set of professionals he had hired to train the seventeen-year-old Anaya. The meeting lasted for an hour and at the end of it, Shariff was made aware that Anaya was in a relationship with her thirty-seven-year-old female physical trainer. Surprised that one of the best, trusted and youngest of the professionals could do such a thing, Shariff asked, "Are you saying that Anaya is having a physical relationship with her female trainer?"

The Korean mercenary leader replied, "Yes, after our conversation, I caught them together. But you don't have to worry about it; I have taken care of her," he said referring to the female trainer.

Shariff was in a dilemma. His whole plan to toughen her up and become a human killing machine was disintegrating in front of his eyes. When he went to confront Anaya in the two by two cell which she called home, she walked up to him, gave him a hug, and said, "I missed you, Chachu."

However, Shariff was furious and pushed her aside asking, "What are you doing, Noori?" He had almost forgotten that he had buried Noori long ago, and that now she was Anaya.

"Oh! You mean that female trainer? Ahhh, that's not a big deal, Chachu."

The response evoked rage in Shariff and as he tried to slap her, she ducked aside and swiftly twisted his hand, forcing him to face the steel wall with a thump. Her hold was strong and in fact proved too much for an army officer like him.

"Chachu, please don't give me any reason to hurt you. I am not a toy anymore!" Her action was more like a trained stealth commando. The fact dawned on him that Anaya was now fully capable of looking after herself.

"I did what I had to do to gain leverage in this awful training. I was being suppressed by everyone, my entire life, even you. I needed my freedom, freedom to eat what I felt, freedom to sleep. I needed that freedom to live my life the way I wanted," Anaya stopped for a breath.

"But there was no way out. So I chose this way to achieve my freedom, I needed someone on my side. Inside this cell, I saw only Jun lee hue was lonely and vulnerable."

"I satisfied her to get what satisfied me. It was just a simple give and take equation, that's all, and of course, I faked it each time."

Shariff was amazed to discover how futile his worries had been. Anaya was already quite conniving. Then she asked another question, "Since we are talking like two adults now, tell me how K.A. Niazi is related to me? He is the puzzle I need to solve first."

Shariff was again dumbstruck by her intelligence and her curiosity, but eventually relented and said, "He is your father." There was no change in Anaya's body language.

Shariff then proceeded to narrate the whole story about Niazi – his days of glory, his downfall as he double-crossed his nation and the people responsible for his fate like R.K. Rao.

Shariff had visualized the day many times in his mind when he would reveal her identity. He had envisioned Anaya seething in anger. However, there stood a calm Anaya in front of his eyes. Anaya also noticed his reaction and broke her silence.

"Were you expecting me to react to that? Sorry, I cannot. Knowing that Niazi is my father and what had happened to him, I only feel pity for him. To be frank, the man got what he deserved!"

Hearing the same harsh words that Rao had said to him once, filled Shariff with a deep anger. His palm shot out and landed on Anaya's cheek, not once, but three times, when suddenly he realized that she could have stopped that. This thought was broken by the next words she uttered.

"See how angry you are, Chachu?"

Shariff was quite in awe. "I lived with that anger every day of my life. Now I am able to rise above it. I am not interested to know, why you and my monstrous father killed so many men, women, and children back in those days. My only interest lies in knowing what did I do to deserve this new me and this dark cold cell?" Shariff realized that Anaya clearly did not remember her own agonizing childhood.

Then Shariff narrated her own sordid childhood, summarizing it with, "Otherwise, why would Rao decided to hand you back to me. It was Rao's final hit on your father's face, but the wound was stamped on his daughter's womanhood."

A terrible cry broke his narration and he looked back to see Anaya with her hands on her ears. She kept banging her head with the agony of all the past details coursing through her mind vividly. Shariff tried to stop her and could not. Finally, she collapsed unconscious to the floor.

Once she came back to her senses, she got up and walked to the small window looking out into the garden with its yellow trees and a pond full of geese.

That was then. They did not meet each other until she turned twenty-one and was back on English soil.

Six

The Red, Acquaintance

The man standing near the defibrillator filled adrenaline in an injection and threw it towards Bulla, who supposed to catch the injection. But he was distracted by the latest reading on the defibrillator.

"What?" he muttered.

Bulla was shocked to realize that Arya was not dead. At that exact time, Arya caught the injection and plunged it right into Bulla's heart. Arya then proceeded to administer the same injection to the man sitting next to him. The man started shaking in pain. Unsteady on his feet, Arya walked up to the third man standing near the defibrillator. He swung two nodes of high voltage wire towards him. One live wire hit his right hand and the other hit him on his left leg. There was a crackle of electricity and fire. Arya pinned him down with his leg, took out his semi-automatic gun, and shot him in the head.

Splashing some water on his face, he turned the corner to find Zehana. She was lying lifeless on the desk. Her expression was peaceful. Arya vowed that Zehana's death would not go in vain, he lightly kissed her on the forehead, covered her body with a piece of cloth, and left.

Arya checked his Smith & Wesson double action, 0.45 ACP, semi-automatic weapon, for any bullets. There were eight bullets in each rack, which was probably enough, he thought.

Arya found his shirt, cleaned the blood spots from his face and tried to look normal. He opened the door slightly and saw a long transit ahead, with steel railings on both sides. He had to find Aisha, and get back to base. Arya formed a plan in his head. He peered through the small windows in each room. The first few rooms had little girls of different ethnicity, lying on the floor, hands bruised with needle marks. It was clear Mir was running his own brothel.

After a brief search, he ascertained that Aisha was not there, dead or alive. Through one of the toilet windows, he leaped himself out in open. When Arya reached the main street from the alley, he suddenly realized that the interrogation chamber was built below the Syrian Consulate. He retraced his path with a new realization – Mir was immensely well connected and had powerful people backing him.

Arya struggled to stand on his feet while navigating himself back to the base. The sign on the door indicated it to be closed in Turkish. Farooq usually did this whenever Virat had to have some meeting with the team. He shouted for Farooq, but there came no answer. With great difficulty, Arya climbed down the stairs only to stumble and fall on the last few steps. As he lay face down on the ground, groaning with pain and wishing for someone to come and help him, he realized no one was available. He slowly turned his face towards the ceiling. The place was empty and bare. There were no laptops, no charts. Arya wondered whether it was cleaned intentionally or had the location been compromised. The pain was unbearable now and he had to do something. Luckily, the medicine box was in its rightful place. It had all the essential items he needed.

He had done this routine before – first take on the yellow one, then the red one followed by the grey one without any water. Then he sat on the stool, took out the syringe, and injected himself. These medicines were specially developed by his agency for such conditions and were a combination of opium and opioid. These were extremely effective drugs, but they had side effects and caused unbearable pain. Arya roared with pain, which was unbearable. His right hand started shaking continuously and he started slapping the desk in front of him furiously with his left hand, probably to feel something more than this annoying pain. Few seconds was all it lasted; the pain was almost gone. It was as if someone had given him his life back.

Although it was his first touch of her pale skin with his fingers at her midriff, it felt immensely pleasing. Her skin was soft like silk. Arya felt weak and unable to stop himself right there and continued to kiss her T-shaped belly button. His kisses increased in intensity and he could hear her moaning erotically. At first, he was gentle, but the more he kissed her belly, the more he felt eager to kiss more passionately. Her engaging erotic voice was inviting. With every touch, their bodies heated up further. She forced Arya to kiss her breasts. He could feel her body lifting up in the air with an erotic sigh. With his swift touch and smooth approach, she lost control and wrapped her legs around Arya's waist. Her grip was strong and she definitely indicated that she was ready for him. Arya then lifted her, head tilted backward and her arms on the ground supporting their position. Arya now started kissing her beautiful neck. She did not object. The first kiss on her lower neck felt strong and tasted like blood.

What!

His partner had a wild cut on her neck and blood was drifting down from her neck through her cleavage.

Fuck! Did I cut her so deep?

A faint moan became louder and louder, breaking the moment and he definitely felt the presence of another woman in the dull room. He felt weak and unable to look for this other woman. And then the faint moan became a devil's laugh. There he was, the devil himself. Mir standing right at the corner, laughing aloud.

Arya threw his mysterious partner on the floor and got up to finish the matter with Mir right there.

However, he wasn't there anymore. Arya turned around to the man clapping. Someone just pulled the ground beneath Arya, because when he saw this man, it was Virat.

What? How…??

Virat was clapping with a smile and gesturing Arya to look at his partner lying in a pool of blood. Arya saw her naked body sprawled across the bed. He ran towards her and grabbed her by her arm. Her hair still covered her face, and he removed them rapidly.

Arya felt as if he had been struck by lightning, as he saw the lifeless eyes of his partner Zehana. He felt dead scared for the first time and threw her back on the ground; he felt dizzy. At the same time, a woman started crying. He opened his eyes again with fear, and there in front of him was Aisha. He certainly could not take it anymore and fell on the floor lifeless, but alive. He felt like he was floating around in the air. Aisha was standing right above him, weeping tears of blood.

Arya woke up from the scariest dream with a scream, breathing heavily. He quickly scanned the surroundings. He had been unconscious in the bathtub.

After shaking himself out of his dream, he found no clue whatsoever at the base which could lead him to his teammates, He needed answers and quickly.

The only option left to him was Farooq. Not standard protocol, but desperate times need desperate measures. Farooq lived in an old flat on the third floor of a building near the bars, just round the corner.

He heard the loud squeal of tires, then brakes, from outside the bar. He peeked out; it seemed like the Turkish police.

Dear god, how had this happened? How did they know this location? Tanveer?

Arya slipped out through the open fire door and raced up the basement stairs of the building next door. As he ran, he caught a glimpse of two or three Nissan Navara D40 covering the front. It was the Turkish police, with Turkish Intelligence.

This time he knew his exit.

He was short of breath, but he coursed with adrenaline and barely stopped to think or grasp air. He had to get to Farooq's apartment and connect with the others.

It was an old studio apartment; Farooq had applied all the security measures in this apartment. He wasn't home but the old guy meant it when he prattled about all new age technologies in his house that could be utilized as a secondary measure if the base was compromised.

They had a perfect plan to start with – they knew that once they got Marcos, the man who created that microdot, they could flush out Mir. Why then all of a sudden were bits and pieces scattered all over? To top it all, he found himself frustrated and unable to rearrange the pieces to understand what happened to him and his team on that rainy night of Monday, the 12th of September.

When it all started and went awry.

Seven

The Red, Emissary

Tanveer entered the apartment and closed the door slowly. He then placed all the groceries on the table. After taking out the bread, he took out a knife to slice it. He suddenly turned around and threw the knife at the man behind him, pointing a gun at his back. He had sensed someone's presence. This distracted the man for a second and Tanveer was swift to take his gun out from under the dinner table. He fired it at him without thinking for a second. His gun made a clinched sound, which meant the gun was empty.

Tanveer smiled at him, still pointing to the empty gun, "Getting smarter by the day, my friend."

"Find a better spot next time; it's an old-school thing!"

"Very well. But how did you…" Before Tanveer could finish, Arya replied.

"You did your best, with installing the new electronic lock at the door with the same model, and everything. However, what you did not know was that Farooq had changed the sequence in the number pad… changed the position of # and a *, which was only known to Virat and me other than him," replied Arya.

"Then, why didn't you run?" asked Tanveer.

"Let's just say I was desperate. Where is Virat?"

"Ah! Virat, don't you know?" Tanveer said with a disgusted face.

Arya pushed a chair and pointed at him to sit down on it. Tanveer was not responding.

Arya swung hard with his gun and knocked Tanveer on the forehead to throw him on to the floor. Arya sat on his chest and spoke again through clenched teeth. "Tanveer, don't even think for a second that I would hesitate to finish you here. I just want you to answer me."

"Oh yeah… I know your questions… first, where is your team leader, and the second, the most interesting one, why the CIA and the RAW are trying to hunt you down right now?"

Arya thought he had heard something wrong. CIA? How did they come into the picture? Surely RAW was not hunting for him because if they did, they would have captured him at the base where he was unconscious for hours. But then again, Tanveer knew something, something far worse than his own situation of being nearly killed by Mir, so he played along.

"Enlighten me," said Arya

Arya grabbed Tanveer's shirt collar with one hand and hauled him up, making him sit on the chair again.

Tanveer started to snigger.

"Okay… let me tell you a story."

Monday, 12ᵗʰ September
Close to Alacati Izmir's, Old City of Izmir
7 p.m.

Virat was pissed at you for following your wild hunch. He sensed you being lured purposely, so he didn't wait any further. We raided the warehouse. Killing every guard swiftly, we advanced to Marco's location. However, it never crossed our minds that one of them could do something unthinkable. Instead of firing at us, the last standing guard fired a shot at Marcos. Surely, they were instructed to do so. The guards were not safeguarding him; they were there to break the link between Marcos and Mir.

Marcos was dead. We felt frustrated, and time was slipping from our hands. At first, we all saw the genius Virat was. He searched the whole place and derived a conclusion that Mir had headed off to Budapest. He convinced the entire team that Mir was meeting his masters to fetch a crooked plan such as 26/11. The team then headed to Budapest that night, leaving me here to clean up the mess and find you.

"That sly bastard! How could he do that to me!" Arya felt Tanveer being genuinely upset.

"Do you know why the CIA wants your head? That bugger not only broke all protocol while killing Mir, but also assassinated nine random people.

"I don't know the details, but the way my agency is being pushed by the CIA to hunt anyone from RAW out in the open, I feel those random people were either CIA or some high-value assets of theirs.

"RAW wanted revenge, but the plan botched up when their own pawn screwed up the mission. To add to the misery, he left pieces of evidence of his presence, connecting everything to RAW," Tanveer concluded.

"But why?"

"You knew him better? Do you think he is some lunatic assassin? The harshness of this job can push anybody to their limits, and there is no defined time or period for it. Maybe it was his time; he always looked on the edge." Arya agreed for a moment.

Tanveer chuckled, "I feel he planned his early retirement on that very spot."

There was a tense silence for a while before Arya could gather himself. The situation had turned out to be far worse than he could have ever imagined. He being framed for all this nonsense?

Tanveer spoke again.

"I pity you. Either you were involved in the plot from the start or you were being played, like me. I know how you must be feeling – betrayed. Your superiors should have thought it through before unleashing that whacker. If you ask me, you were dead the minute you signed up for this job. A new recruit like yourself is always destined to be bait. They put you in the field explaining some patriotic shit and if anything goes wrong, you will be served on a platter."

Judging Arya's silence, Tanveer played his trump card.

"I suggest you surrender yourself to me, maybe we can have a deal for you with the Americans."

There is no such thing as a 'friend' in this line of work. Everyone helps each other for their means, Shubhendu had always instructed him.

For a moment or two, Arya actually thought about the easy way out, ready to sell his loyalty to stay alive.

A phone rang near the bed of the studio apartment. For a split second on reflex, Arya got distracted and removed his gaze from Tanveer.

Tanveer assessed the golden chance. Arya lost the possession of his gun with that first blow. Tanveer landed a few punches on Arya's face and a powerful kick to his gut.

The kick threw Arya on the dinner table and then flipping over to the floor. Before Arya could assemble himself back, Tanveer positioned himself carefully behind and started choking Arya to death. The deadly chokehold pushing Arya to unconsciousness.

The phone was still ringing shrilly and its continuous ringing snapped something in Arya's brain.

Arya gathered his whole energy to stand up. He grabbed Tanveer's hand which was choking him and twisted it. He then proceeded to lift Tanveer off the ground. With Tanveer on his back, he hit the window edge with a force. Tanveer felt the pain and the grip on his neck eased a bit which was sufficient for a trained operative to grab the essential oxygen.

Before Tanveer could grab him back, Arya started to punch Tanveer in his ribs with his elbow.

Tanveer saw Arya breathing heavily upright a few metres away from him. They were both silent, contemplative of their next move. The table had many tools they could use, so they made a run for it. Tanveer got hold of a kitchen knife and Arya could only manage to pick up a spoon.

Tanveer had his laugh and said, "A spoon?"

Arya roared, "Let's just get on with it!"

Tanveer moved towards Arya first. He swung the sharp-edged knife, angling to cut Arya's throat. Arya bent down a little and shoved his spoon towards Tanveer's ribs. The spoon hit the exact place where Arya intended to. Tanveer was shocked with the pain, and soon realized Arya had a fork in his hand. Tanveer felt a little frustrated looking at his opponent who was now calm as ice.

Arya's next few strategic moves confirmed he would not be an easy target. Tanveer ran wild, swinging his knife to cut Arya. Arya now knew he had an edge because he could see the frustration in Tanveer's moves; the more frustrated your opponent gets, the easier it is to target them. Arya let the first few swings go by to estimate Tanveer's timing. He then caught the fourth swing, twisted his wrist and stabbed it with the fork. Tanveer lost his knife.

Arya did not waste much time to neutralize Tanveer, who was still unsuccessful to land even a punch at the right spot. Tanveer sucked himself into Arya's web, being stabbed in his elbows, fingers, ribs and other parts of the body. All it took were a few seconds. Tanveer's eyes were forlorn, trashed on the floor. Arya sat next to him, grabbing his neck tightly with one hand and pulling his hair with another.

"Till the last blood in my vein, I will not be a traitor."

He had a faraway look as he said, "I do not believe that either my company or my superiors plotted this assassination. And if they did…" He chewed his words before speaking, "Then help me, god! I will find each of them and kill them piece by piece."

◆

Few moments later, the apartment blew up in flames, enough to shatter the windows and doors. The evidence linking the apartment to a safehouse was destroyed soon after Arya drove away with the wounded soul. Arya and Tanveer saw a local police car crossing them, one by one with their emergency sirens on, followed by firefighters and an ambulance.

"It still doesn't change anything between us, Tanveer. I saved your life only because I am not trained to kill anyone who questions my motives. You are in my debt, which can be a complicated place to be," Arya said and drove away, leaving Tanveer at nearby medical center.

The best foot forward was to gain some of the trust back from his own agency RAW. To do so, he would have to make a contact. He had never met the Brigadier in person; all he knew was a code name with which he could be contacted. To the best of his knowledge and understanding, the Brigadier must be the most important piece in this chain, thus he was an emergency contact.

"Can I have a beer? A cheap one?" Arya requested the bartender after occupying the farthest corner chair. From his position, he could keep an eye on everyone through the rack glass behind the bartender.

"Here you go," the bartender placed a glass of chilled beer on a napkin expressionlessly.

This bar had blue radium lights all over the ceiling, which made everyone look like a blue monster. As soon as Arya gulped a big sip of that beer, he felt good. He thought this beer was not so cheap in taste and couldn't resist taking a few more swigs and ordered one more round of the same. He then lit a cigarette and took brief and long puffs. Arya felt an instant kick to think about what to do next, because one wrong move from here would get him killed. It would also disown the credibility of Indian intelligence forever. He remembered the conversation he had had with the Brigadier's personal assistant Mrs Hegde just a while ago. The Brigadier must be in tremendous pressure to handover the emergency protocol to his secretary.

"You bunch of bitchy little girls put up a marvellous show on the mission which was supposed to be a covert OP. RAW has been put under scrutiny by PMO, headed by Dr Subramanian, a bureaucrat," Mrs Hegde spat in anger, without interruption for a second.

"I know, Mrs Hegde, that things look dim, but you have to convince Brigadier that I am not a traitor." Arya's voice was firm and single pitched.

"Oh... boy! Don't sell me the crap. That you aren't a part of it and Virat double-crossed you? If that's the case, my boy, for this sole reason, you're being paid and trained for!"

Her voice literally tore off Arya's hearing.

After a brief silence Arya spoke again, "Every one of us is on the edge here. It's time for us to make things right again, and believe me, I am going to do exactly that, with or without RAW."

"Okay... you realize what you are asking me to do, right? We can't have things connecting back to us; you will be disposed of if caught!"

"Aren't we always?" Arya chuckled.

"I will pass your message to the Brigadier, and keep an eye on Budapest."

"But how will you reach there? I mean..." She knew it was nearly impossible for Arya to make his way out of Turkey, especially without RAW support.

'Can a new recruit be trusted so much?' she thought.

"You let me worry about that. Please get me a solid contact who can get me the moon if I ask for it!"

Mrs Hegde hung up, agreeing to the demand.

Nine

The Red, Beauty

Arya was onto his third round of the same cheap beer. In his mind, he was constantly searching for someone who could provide him with a safe passage to Budapest. This was one of the most important reasons why a new recruit is never sent alone on a mission. Lack of good local contacts. Your own contacts not only help you to achieve your mission, but sometimes help you survive on foreign soil. A new recruit like Arya had a disadvantage in this section; he had barely started teething and found himself with his mouth full of things to chew.

He suddenly remembered Shubhendu's iconic words of wisdom, *"Beta tum bar bar Govardhan parvat kyun uthane lag jaate ho?"*

Remembering those words made him chuckle. He had come close to only one asset, and she was Aisha. With that thought, he gulped down the last drop of beer, when his instinct alerted him. Someone just went past him to the exit. He glanced for a reflection on the glass case on the wall, but missed whoever it was.

◆

A woman came out of Erc-Bar in a hurry. She was dressed in an overcoat and trousers, with a scarf on her head. Her left hand held a small purse and her right hand was inside it as if she was holding on to something important. Judging by her watchful nature and fast stride, she seemed frightened. She reached for the handle of her car, but before she could open the door, she felt someone breathing behind her back. She swayed her arms free from her purse, and a Beretta.22 swung to point on the suspicious man behind her.

The man behind wasn't a newbie and saw it coming, so he jabbed her wrist. She lost control of her Beretta.22, even before she could turn and see his face. The man grabbed her wrist, turned her towards him, and before she knew it, he forced her towards the car.

Bamm!

The force was so hard that the car lilted back and forth and a cry came out of her. This man was seriously furious with her. She was grabbed from all corners, and couldn't move an inch. The man and the lady came face-to-face for the first time. They both stood still, watching each other suspiciously, their eyes widening with the realization that they knew each other.

"Do you mind?" the woman spoke first, catching a short breath.

"Yes, in fact, I do, Aisha." Arya stood firm not allowing her to move an inch. "Why are you following me?"

Aisha replied with a puzzled look, "You have bad breath. Did you drink too much? Last time I checked, you were following me!" With frustration she spoke again, "Do you mind loosening your grip, you are making me uncomfortable?"

Arya thought for a moment, stepping aside.

"I... I was, but..." she stopped in the middle of her sentence, looked at someone far away, heading towards them.

Arya also looked at the man walking, and closing in fast.

"This place is not safe. Could you please pass me the gun? I should leave and suggest you leave as well."

"I need a place to stay for the night."

"Yeah, sure...." She responded as if Arya had just cracked a joke.

"Like you have a choice!" Arya replied, showing that he still possessed her Berretta, and slipped into the back seat of the car. Looking at her limited options, she also sat on the driver's seat and drove away.

Before taking a turn onto the main road, she and Arya looked back at the man who by then stood at the exact spot where Aisha had parked, watching them disappear.

After a mile or two, Arya glanced back to see if anyone was following them. No one. This hour of the day was very easy to pick up a tail. "So you were saying?" Arya broke the silence in the car.

Aisha replied looking at the rearview mirror, "I was saying what? Oh yes... I have a distant cousin from my mother's side. We met a few months back when I was shopping. I was not aware of his existence until that day. His name is Razeeq. He smuggles goods, antiques, people, so basically, anything that can be smuggled."

Then she stopped to catch her breath.

"So?" Arya wanted her to continue. Instead of continuing, she put her foot on the brakes so hard that the car skidded, moved forward for a good five metres and then finally stopped. She knew what she was doing; she controlled herself but Arya's head hit the front passenger seat, jerked back and forward.

Before he could speak, Aisha pulled her scarf off, and turned to Arya and spoke,

"Listen, you..."

When she spoke in a rush, she was also careful about not ruining her cherry red lipstick. Even when she was on the run for her life, she was able to find time to put artificial eyelashes on her ocean blue eyes. The eyes of a goddess.

"Are you listening to me, and stop staring at me like this?"

"Yes, yes... So where were you?" This was the second time that Arya felt weak in front of her charming beauty.

"I said I am not your driver, so bring your ass in the front seat and would you mind keeping the gun down! I am not going to bite you."

They drove for about an hour and reached a place near the shore. It was a not-so-posh neighbourhood. She lived in a one-bedroom apartment all by herself – with a floor bedding, an open plan kitchen and living space, and a small but clean bathroom. Aisha went straight to the bathroom.

Arya went to the window, and looked outside for any suspicious car or some sort of danger; he found nothing out of the ordinary.

She came out after a good half an hour in her sleeping suit made of red silky fabric. Her makeup was off, but she was wearing her red lipstick. It was clear that red was her favourite colour and it suited her well. She had tied her hair neatly.

"So what's with you? I see you have made it alive from the embassy," she spoke putting some sort of moisturizer on her arms in front of the mirror.

"It's a long story, listen I appreciate all your help. As the day dawns, I will be on my way."

Looking at his direct approach, she said, "Suit yourself. After all, you have saved my life and I never got a chance to say thank you. We are even! "

Arya nodded. He had very little money left in his pocket since RAW had frozen his account and declined to acknowledge his existence as an Indian. Aisha enquired, "Are you hungry? I am making an omelette for myself."

"No, I am good," he said as she placed the pan on the stove and broke two eggs and cut some cheese, onions and tomatoes.

Few seconds later, she explained her side of the story. She was in the bar as her smuggler cousin had instructed her to pick up papers, but no one had showed up. When she called him, he barked like a dog.

"Can you believe him, my own cousin?"

With these last words, she made her eyes as big as possible. Her omelette was ready by then and she started eating it from the pan. She, again, did not care to finish her side of the story. She finished the omelette in three or four bites and then spoke with her mouth full.

"So I hurried out of the bar, and you slammed me!"

She was clearly looking for an apology.

Arya didn't care to respond since he was very tired from all the running, thinking and twisting his head. He headed towards the floor bed.

Aisha interrupted him by saying, "Where do you think you are going, Mister?"

Arya gave her a glare and picked up one pillow, took the sheet, which was covering the mattress and moved towards the wall next to the bathroom. He then sat on the floor kept the pillow behind him, and closed his eyes.

He overheard Aisha saying "Unbelievable!"

Arya didn't sleep for a while, but he didn't open his eyes either. He realized after a while that Aisha had fallen asleep on her bed. As midnight approached, Arya's mind shut down automatically.

A dog barked on the street, which alerted Arya to his senses. He woke up and found his hand still tightened on the gun. He quickly scanned the room from where he sat. He had a clear sight of the bed on the floor and next to it was the only route to enter or exit in the apartment. The room was almost dark, but he could clearly make out that Aisha wasn't in her bed, so he alerted his senses to see if the lady was in the bathroom. Nope, no sound. From his position, only one part of the apartment was not visible, the part which had the windows. It was blocked by the divider created to give a feel that this apartment had a kitchen as well. He tilted his head and what he saw mesmerized him. He saw Aisha.

She was sitting on a stool, leaning against the wall near the window, looking out. Half of her face shining in the moonlight. She had folded one leg on the stool and the other one stretched out far. The window was lit up and Arya could see her astonishing beauty. She had an anklet with little stars on her ankle. He saw her talking a sip from a glass, filled with some brown sparkling liquid and some ice – a scotch. The woman was resourceful and her charm could spell magic when she showed desperation through her ocean blue eyes. He admired that aspect. A sudden breeze coming in from the shore made the atmosphere pleasant. The breeze also made her half-buttoned shirt flap like a kite. Arya caught a glimpse of her figure, the area near her navel was well crafted and her peach coloured skin had the same glow as her face. The long scar on her lower back ended at her waistline. No one could guess by looking at her perfect figure that she was in her forties; she had a body of a twenty-year-old. Only her face had some signs of her true age. Arya noticed a drop of tear trickle down from her shut eyes. Was she crying? Nope, her lips were tilted upwards. She was smiling in her thoughts, far from being sad or worried about her life. She must be feeling alive and free again after a while since she slipped out of the hands of Mir, the bastard. Arya was completely spellbound when she turned towards him and caught him staring at her. He kept eye contact; she winced, and her eyebrows shot up questioningly, "What?"

Arya just nodded. She stretched her arm, holding the scotch as if offering it to him. Arya again declined. She went back to the way she was, staring out. The mature woman didn't show any emotional sign that she cared. Arya thought it would be best to close his eyes again.

When he finally woke up, it was about ten in the morning. His gaze was fixed on Aisha. She was near the same window, reading the newspaper. She had the same position on the stool; her morning coffee was on the ledge. She was in a loose T-shirt and it was the only piece of clothing she cared to wear. He was helpless again and his eyes ignored his every command. The morning was turning brighter with her in his sight.

By the third day, another problem rose. They were running out of groceries. Arya decided to step outside for some. It was about quarter past eight in the evening when he returned.

He was near the door when he heard the thump of someone hitting the ground hard. Then came a faint moan. He rushed to door, to find it unlocked but chained from inside. Through the slit, he could see Aisha on the ground, moaning on the floor. She was not wearing her bottoms and her shirt's buttons were undone. He drew his gun from the grocery bag, fixing the gun at the narrow space between the door and its bracket. He needed this to be discreet, so he waited. Within seconds, he saw a man coming into view. The man was looking at helpless Aisha like a prey. A bullet sound came out from Arya's gun. He had taken a head shot, but since he didn't have the luxury of a clear vision and space, the bullet hit the burglar's throat. He was on the ground holding his neck, and didn't have a chance to scream or even shriek. Aisha looked at the door and when she saw Arya's familiar eyes peeking in, she ran wildly to open it. She hugged him tight and he could feel her heart pounding like a piston through her bosom. Arya grabbed her and came inside, closing the door first.

The now dead man was nearly six feet tall, medium built with curly hair and a broad chin with a stubble and a heavy moustache. He appeared to be a local.

"Do you recognize him?" Arya inquired as he knelt down beside the dead man, scanning him closely and checking his pockets for a clue. Aisha didn't respond, still weeping. His wallet had no identity card, just had some money. That frustrated Arya.

He stood up, grabbed Aisha with both arms and shook her to get some answers out.

"How... do you know him?"

She threw a puzzled face "No... no... I don't!"

"Then why the hell did you let him in?" his voice had a suspicious tone.

"He... he said he was Razeeq's friend and had come with the groceries, that... ammm..."

Arya spoke hurriedly again, "And you said come, come on in. And have some scotch. You bloody..."

His tone was sceptical and taunting. She was pleading for some empathy in his eyes, but there was none. She turned red and spoke, "Do you think that I wanted all of this? Or do you think I love being raped repeatedly?"

She forced Arya's gun and pointed it towards her bosom, *"Set me free! Do it!"* she screamed her guts out.

There was a murderous silence after that cry; Arya looked at those closed eyes. A drop of blood skidded down from the side of her lips to her chin. Arya thought he was getting honey-trapped – a very useful and common tool in the field of espionage. Sometimes a spook like him also tends to forget that there are real people in this world and they are as innocent as Aisha. She opened her teary eyes finally. Arya drew his gun away from her and cleaned the blood on her chin with his thumb.

"Put on something. I think it's time to meet your cousin."

During the drive, he asked, "How did you manage to escape alive from Mir's captivity?"

"I had a sympathizer. He was one of the many men Mir had on me, all the time. I don't know why, but he helped me escape that night. I don't know why he chose that day when he could have saved me earlier with all those...." her voice trembled. "Can we not talk about any of those please?"

With a blurry vision, she opened her eyes to a beautiful sunny day without him on the driving seat. Her body ached. Aisha rolled her head to search for him.

"Coffee?" he offered while sipping his.

He was standing outside resting his back against the car. Arya kept watch on the house the whole night. No movement at all. He needed to be sure before meeting Razeeq.

Razeeq was of smaller build than Arya had imagined. He had the face of a scum. He was in hiding, and it took a lot for Arya and Aisha to convince him that they were not here to kill him. He looked paranoid and kept on abusing Aisha with a shotgun pointed at Arya initially. After much struggle, Arya convinced him to stay calm.

"The day... I waaasss... supposed to meet, A... A... A... A... A... Aisha at the bar," finally, when he spoke a full sentence, Arya understood he had a stammering issue, and his paranoia made it more difficult.

"It's all because of this bitch!"

"Hey asshole, I swear, I'll kill you first if you abuse her one more time."

Arya turned to Aisha and said, "Aisha, go out, and wait."

Some local rival, who had political connections in Turkey, was targeting Razeeq. Razeeq's men were either murdered or made a run for it, leaving him alone. It was a mere case of a gang war. If what Razeeq had been saying was true, he would not survive this war, so he had gone into hiding. His rival not only had connections with the political lobby, but also seemed to have the local police in his pocket. The last time he had tried to help Aisha escape, it was horrible. He was nearly killed by his rivals.

Arya needed his services, but to get that, he needed to settle Razeeq back into his business.

"It's me Tanveer, and I am in desperate need of your help," Arya said over the phone.

Tanveer couldn't be trusted at all with Arya's escape, but he could be lured into clearing the mess Razeeq was in. After all, he belonged to a National Intelligence Organization of Turkey, and Arya had a trump card over him.

"Look, my friend, I really can't help you here. What you are asking me will kill my career. The guy you are after may well be our next home minister."

"Tanveer, there is no easy way to say this, but you have to choose between your career and your family today."

The hint was enough for Tanveer to sense where this talk was heading. A series of abuses were hurled at Arya.

"You do this for me, and I promise to burn all the evidence against you."

"That sly bastard Virat, that motherfucker..." Tanveer understood Virat had shared all the evidence with Arya. Arya's bluff paid off.

"So I take this as a yes. You are going to help me in this?"

"You godforsaken bastard? But why are you helping some random guy?"

"I have my reasons."

Arya cleared his throat and told Tanveer, "So this is what you are going to do..."

Thus followed the series of instructions given to Tanveer by his new handler. Spies will use whatever they can, to get behind enemy lines – stealth, deception, even blackmail. One great thing about politicians is, wherever you go, they all are the same. The more famous a politician is, nine out of ten will have more skeletons in their cupboard. Later in the day, Tanveer found something useful, and the decisive plan took place in an hour. With the politicians out of the equation, Razeeq's rival was alone against two agency spies – Arya and Tanveer. In a matter of a day, Razeeq's rival was running to save his own sorry ass for survival.

Razeeq hugged Arya tightly. His eyes were moist.

"My contact will smuggle you to a small coastal city called Pula in Croatia from Turkey. Once you are in Pula, I can provide you with a car and with important papers which will help you to get into Budapest by driving six hours through Zagreb. Here are the other items you asked for."

By the night of 19th September, they were on their way to Budapest.

Ten

The Red Spy Craft

23rd September
Budapest, Hungary

Gopal Mahato was the First Secretary of the Indian embassy in Budapest, Hungary. He was a true diplomat with higher political aspirations and contacts in the Hungarian political administration, which continued to its neighbouring countries. He was born and brought up in a village near Ranchi back in India. The man who looked older than his actual age, as a matter a fact, had turned fifty.

Being a man with such influence, he looked worried with a mystified grim face. He and the Ambassador were taking the direct heat not only from US, but also from their friends in Hungarian politics as well. By every hour, things were getting rather obvious to him, that he was being watched 24x7. He almost had his heart in his mouth, when Mrs Hegde asked him to facilitate the man from RAW. He couldn't refuse the order. He was one of them, not directly pay-rolled, but positioned strategically with the help of RAW as 2nd in command of Hungary.

She specially emphasised he visit the Hindu Vaishnava Temple in Budapest. However, as ordered, he visited the temple. And since then, it had been a tiring, odd, brainstorming, nervous day for him. From the mandir's pandit to a fruit seller, and from the fruit seller to a tour guide, and from him to so many other people he met during the whole day as he was handed some rather obvious clues or a note saying what he would do for the next hour. Like there was a note for him handed over when he got the prasad at the temple, which read:

My apologies for the whole day in advance, but you would have to do exactly as I say. I am from RAW. Act as normal as possible, take calls, inform your office that you want to enjoy the whole day and only be back in office by five in the evening. Tell your driver to go and have your car serviced and you will enjoy public transport today. Your next stop will be a fruit store near the temple and you must buy lots of apples. Let me assure you, you will have a wonderful time today, sir."

He continued getting clues after clues at very obvious but well-hidden places within the surroundings so that it seemed that he was actually enjoying his birthday. In the afternoon, he got a sudden call from his son that he wanted to have lunch at Pizza Hut; he went there only to find his next clue awaiting him and his schedule for the next hour. At some point, he thought someone must have been playful, but as the day progressed, the clues explained to him how many men were following him and how they were changing cars and shifts to follow him discreetly. Whoever was the man, he definitely was sharp and had an orthodox method! Mr Gopal couldn't believe that he actually went on a roller coaster ride at the age of 50, but he followed every instruction obediently. The last clue got him back to the Indian Embassy.

Anyway, since he didn't receive any more clues, it was time to head home.

"Ashok, it's hot in here, bring down the heater." His driver saw him sweating in the cold winter of Budapest.

"Are you alright sir?" his driver enquired, but got no answer.

Gopal was sweating, because he had got the last note hidden in the car seat. A paper napkin with an address. He had to loosen his tie, he felt as if he needed a little more oxygen to breathe and calm himself down. Gopal screamed from inside, "Have they totally lost it? Why the f*** do they need a blueprint of CIA's headquarters?"

The instruction read the information to be stored on a pen drive, and dropped in a garbage box near his house by the next morning.

◆

At the corner of the high profile diplomatic area where Gopal lived, a car entered at full speed and stopped at a distance from Gopal's house. The driver and the other two passengers watched carefully as Gopal walked into the house.

"Dave, I think something is wrong here," the driver of that Alfa Romeo 159 spoke suspiciously to his fellow passenger. He had a semi-automatic Mp5 with a silencer on him.

He responded, "You are being paranoid, Chuck. This man is perfectly normal. I am tired of following this guy around. I just want to go home to my beautiful wife." He looked exhausted. The third man in the passenger seat was John J. Mikhail, who by appearance was American, but had an odd accent that hinted at him spending a lot of time in European countries.

"It's too odd to be a coincidence, I mean the whole day? Mikhail, I think we should report this to Madelyn." His last words were affirmative and commanding. Dave was the only one to object, "Suit yourself, but you know the bitch. She hates the fools around her more than she hates her enemy. If this doesn't pay off, she is going to stick her finger up in our asses."

Mikhail was hesitant for a moment, but being the senior officer at the scene he called the CIA headquarters and explained his suspicions to Madelyn Hunter, and gave a briefing. After a pause, she ordered them to stay put.

Far away on the same street from Dave, Chuck and Mikhail, a pair of eyes watched them through binoculars and tried to write whatever was grasped through lip reading. Once he wrote down everything on a pad, he looked at the scratchy sentences. He saw exactly what he wanted to see, and he had circled the name, Madelyn Hunter. He was able to get the idea that those three fellows were not going anywhere the whole night.

CIA headquarters
Station Chief, Budapest, Hungary – Madelyn Hunter

Madelyn Hunter ordered to the operations centre analyst down one floor that she wanted him to tap all the phones in Gopal's house, including his wife's, his son's and even their maid's. She felt tired and exhausted, but this was not the time to rest. She sat down on an extra-large chair for her height, crossed both her legs in front of her on her messy desk with an Apple desktop and stared at the AC ventilation. Her mind was running in all directions and she started analysing exactly what had happened since she tasked to lead a team for Mission 'Barátok', meaning 'Friends'.

Two weeks back, she was asked to report at the CIA headquarters in Langley Virginia, to Deputy Director of the CIA Hamilton Murray, another Afro-American in the office, a confidant of the ruling cabinet of the US government. Madelyn remembered how Hamilton explained to her the benefits with the success of the mission, and how this mission had a clearance at a very high level and the knowledge of this was restricted to only a few in the cabinet. Both Hamilton and Madelyn had very high hopes of the operation's success. They literally saw it as their dream ladder. Hamilton saw this as a confirmation to become the head of the CIA, and Madelyn was convinced by him that she would become the most trusted deputy of his in the European region. Hamilton summarized this mission as a necessary step to form an alliance between CIA, SAVAK and the Broker to come to a mutual consent and plan their strategies in Iran.

Madelyn's task was to prepare a safe passage for CIA agents, for their discreet in and out of Budapest. She objected with Hamilton and spoke clearly, "Until I know the whole story, I will not be able to promise the safety of the agents."

He explained how the meeting was planned to go and that was the time when Madelyn came to know that there wass a broker Jan Mohammad Baloch in this deal between the US and SAVAK. He was in the shadows and had declared that if he smelt anything funny, he would cancel the deal and vanish. The broker was clear that this meet would only happen under his conditions and he did not trust anyone, so no wire, no arms, and no spy shit. It was in everyone's best interest that every party will arrive with only their clothes on; they should not carry even their wallets or cell phones. The deal was not to be recorded under any circumstances. He chose his own way of conducting the deal. It would be on a twelve-seater luxury tourist bus. She thought to object instantly to a moving bus, as it would be hard to protect, but she did not. Later she found she might have made her worst career decision. As per the confidential document, Madelyn got the full report of every individual attending the meeting, including the broker. A kind of a one-page biodata including the CIA agents, one of them was the oldest and most valued agent in the CIA. His career can be summarized with covert ops and affairs, then counter-intelligence, counter-terrorism, and lastly opting to be a handler of many handlers, who manage CIA or non-CIA assets in the Middle East. He had all the experience, expertise, but most importantly, he had a vision – vision of a hawk to see things clearly from a distance. That is why the CIA chose Hawk as his preferred code name.

Madelyn and Hawk crossed each other only once before this meet, back in '99, when she was fresh out of recruitment, young and working on an asset development task in Russia just after the Cold War. Madelyn gave Hawk a fair share of recognition in her success in the intelligence community. Although her time with Hawk was very brief in Russia, during those ten days, he mentored her and channelized her rough edges to the maturity of a sensible agent. Madelyn found an irresistible attraction towards Hawk from day one. She always found herself lured towards the roughness of a man rather than his physical attributes. Therefore, once the job was finished, Madelyn and Hawk spent two days somewhere, feeding off each other's desires. Since then, they always avoided each other deliberately out of mutual consent, and as professionals. This meet was set without asking either of them to be in it.

14th September
Budapest Hungary
At CIA safe house, one hour before the meeting

Madelyn walked up to Hawk, who was dressed up like a professor in his late 50s, with grey hair, clean-shaven and with a pair of glasses. She tried to convince him to wear a small wireless mic so that she could listen on to the conversation inside the bus; it was mainly for her own sake to be on top of things. He responded by saying confidently, "Am I too old for this shit Maddy?"

'Maddy'. She almost forgot how good it felt being called Maddy by Hawk. She never allowed anyone else to call her by that name, other than her first man. It was her sense of justice to that short-lived relation.

Madelyn, along with Hawk and two of his team members reached the botanical garden parking lot in a black GMC terrain and waited inside the SUV, the place where the meet was to start. They all noticed that they were not alone, about twenty metres on the left, one maroon Chevrolet SUV was parked with the same number of passengers – four people including the driver, who avoided eye contact. Must be SAVAK. On the dot at 9 a.m., a modified version of Mercedes-Benz bus came into picture. It had a very fine, polished metallic colour bus with stickers all over it. Bulletproof windows with curtains drawn. The bus then beamed its lights twice, to signal them to board. Passengers inside the Chevrolet stepped out of their vehicle first, first sign shown that they are in a mood to talk, and they left their driver and moved towards the bus. All of them looked exactly as per their CIA profile. Two men in their thirties, medium built, a thick-haired set with unshaven faces, looked like twin brothers, and followed their leader, who was in his seventies.

Nasser Bakhtiar was a former director of operations at the Organization of Intelligence and National Security known as SAVAK, until it was dismantled in 1979. SAVAK had been described as Iran's 'most hated and feared institution', because of its practice of torturing and executing opponents. SAVAK couldn't recover in the last thirty years and stayed in the dust. At its peak, SAVAK had as many as 60,000 agents serving in its ranks. Almost all of them who were in Iran at the time of the Iranian Revolution were hunted down and executed. Only a few, those who were outside of Iran, were believed to have survived, and Nasser Bakhtiar was one of them. No one knew of his existence until this broker contacted the CIA and proposed this plan. SAVAK replaced by the 'much larger' SAVAMA, also known as the Ministry of Intelligence and National Security of Iran. The political equations had changed in the last thirty years, and it was clear to some high-ranking old officials of SAVAMA that they definitely needed to revive SAVAK. As a covert organization within an organization, to control every bit of Iran and probably overthrow the government. Nasser was chosen to convince the CIA for this revolution, and get the necessary help. After all, Iran's Mohammad Reza Shah with the help of the United States' Central Intelligence Agency (the CIA) had established SAVAK back in 1957.

Nasser Bakhtiar at his age looked fit and thin with an almost baldpate, but still possessed a thick, grey beard and moustache, neatly trimmed. His gait was straight and confident, having smelt the power which was about to be bestowed to him after a long, exhausting period of disgraceful hiding. Once they boarded, Madelyn confirmed the status to Hamilton. She never saw the broker. Since it was his caravan, she assumed he was already inside and ready to host the meet. Madelyn's task was half done now, and as per instructions, the bus shouldn't be tailed. However, Madelyn had her own way of not following orders, especially when she was not convinced of the order. Apart from her, there was no other soul under her supervision who knew about the meet. She ditched her car nearby, and boarded an unmarked car along with Matt, her trusted reporter and started tailing the bus. She had given a different story to Matt, and he did not raise any questions. The tourist bus roamed the city for five hours without a hiccup, but never stopped at any place, for obvious reasons. The passengers were not so keen to enjoy the architecture or the beauty of Budapest.

Now the bus had stopped at a traffic signal for the last one minute so that it could take a turn and enter its last destination, Bank Street. Between the bus and Madelyn's car, there were three other cars waiting for the same reason.

Madelyn's eye caught the decreasing number at the traffic light. Twenty seconds left to go green, when the driver ahead of hers decided to leave the third place from the bus and successfully took a slow and a sharp turn to be out of the same queue and drove and parked itself along the right side of the bus, near the driver's seat. A Hyundai Accent 2003 early model. She acknowledged that there were only ten seconds left for the green light to go on, when the driver of the traveller bus jumped out and boarded the Hyundai in a hurry and drove off.

Madelyn screamed at Matt, "Catch them!" by pointing to the direction where the black car had gone.

She ran towards the driver's side of the motionless bus. She knew something bad had already happened, but what?

"Hawk... no, no no..." she was murmuring these broken words when she opened the driver's door and felt the dead calm inside. The driver's area was separated by a small door from the rest of the passenger area. She saw a gas shroud lying on the driver's seat, which was a Military Mark V-gas mask. She hopped in and put the shroud on before kicking the small door open and entering the passenger area. Her heart stopped at once and started beating again. The extra-large sofa seats were modified and carefully arranged to face each other, while the last row was in her direction. There was Nassir and his boys in the left seat; next to them was the broker. She found all of the eight members calmly seated – motionless bodies and eyes wide open in anxiety. Her fear came true. All of them were dead, bullet wounds exactly between their eyebrows. However, it was very strange to see none of them showing any signs of struggle as if their whole bodies had been paralyzed. This looked to be the effect of some sort of a nerve gas before the assassin took a bloody headshot. All of them must have seen their end, but couldn't move. This was brutal, vicious and sadistic.

Where was Hawk? The mist was clearing and there he was, on the floor, dead. It seemed he had tried to reach and open the ventilation glass on the roof of the traveller. The assassin had put a bullet in the back of his head. There was nothing left for her to secure or to grab. She caught a glimpse of a mini van about fifty metres away, moving towards the bus with a small satellite antenna on top of it. She grabbed a silencer from her jacket pocket fixed it onto her gun, emptying the first magazine bullet in the back of Hawk's skull, thrashing it into pieces, and did the same to the other CIA associates. They were not recognizable anymore, at least not until the forensics department released the final report, which could be altered with a few favours. The press shouldn't get the whiff of this. She didn't waste any more time. She quickly came out and ran to hide in the nearby alley full of dumpsters. Her eyes were itchy, red and soggy, probably a small amount of the nerve gas had got in, or was she crying?

Her phone flashed Matt's name when she picked it up. Matt spoke nonstop, updating his side of the story,

"Madelyn, I followed them to the Danube river. They ditched the Hyundai at the street under Margaret Bridge, which connects Buda to Pest. I only managed to catch a glimpse before they dived into the river. It seemed they had their wetsuits ready for the dive underwater and looking at their speed, they could be using an underwater scooter. I searched their car, but got nothing. I lost them." Matt sounded disheartened.

"No, we have not," Madelyn calculated something, and then instructed him.

"They wanted us to think like that. They will not take a chance to swim across Danube river to Vienna. You rush to District III and delay any ongoing cruise. Drive alongside the Danube. Go go go..."

District III, Nanasi Way, Danube River

A car skidded before coming to a halt near Matt. Madelyn rushed out of the car, which she had hijacked near Bank Street from some old woman. She was breathless with anxiety.

Before he could start the brief, a call came from their HQ. Matt responded in shock "What? How accurate is their report?"

Madelyn was looking at Matt, anxious to know what the HQ had just updated.

"Local agencies have found bodies floating under the Árpád Bridge, dead in deep diving suits. One man died because his oxygen tank burst open and he drowned. It is early to say, but I think he is one of the two suspects we are after. Nothing found on them to identify them," Matt briefed her. She did not respond, nor did she show any sign of giving further instructions. Therefore, Matt gave his final understanding about the unusual death of the suspects as, "Killing each other was always on the cards, by whomsoever had hired them for an assassination. Both of them must be unaware that they had both got the same instructions to kill each other, so that there won't be any trace left. I wonder whether the gas tank had actually exploded or was it intentionally blown away by the other partner."

Madelyn could not believe that she missed grabbing them alive. The pause was brief, but her mind was running at supersonic speed. She murmured finally.

"Finding them dead under Árpád bridge confirms that they were headed here, but they had nothing on their body – no ticket no passport, no money, which means..." Her eyes sparkled and the dull face had changed instantly; she had got something significant.

"There is a third person, the transporter!"

Eleven

The Red, Devil's Craft

She still remembered the sourness of that heated talk with the Deputy Director of CIA Hamilton Murray, after their mission 'Barátok' went sideways. Not only had she lost one of her dear colleagues during the operation, she was designated as 'impotent' by Hamilton over the video conference. Their dream had now crashed to the ground and aspirations were shattered into pieces. The only way out of this was if she could get the matter straight and Hamilton could crucify the Indian intelligence agency to the ground. The evidence, however, was not so concrete. All they had was one RAW agent (Farooq) in custody, who was believed to be a sleeper agent for a decade or so, and two dead RAW agents (Virat and Ramanna). They could not bury RAW until they had a substantial proof of the whole plan and had the key members of this organization captured. To some extent, Hamilton was convinced of the fact that if this had to be achieved, Madelyn was the only go-to woman. He knew exactly how to pump her, that is why he had had deliberately chosen those words,

"I think you are losing your edge, Madelyn, and becoming impotent for the job."

On the other side, Madelyn would have preferred a dagger to the heart rather than listen to those words from Hamilton.

Today morning, when she got a call from John J. Mikhail tasked to lead the three-man team to monitor Mr Gopal Mahato, he reported that the man was acting strangely, going to places where he had not been since they were tailing him. Being on the field for so long, Madelyn knew it could be the moment she was waiting for since the assassination. She instructed John to keep their tail on and that she would be sending a couple of more agents to join them. She also deployed the Web to their location in five minutes.

The Web is usually a vehicle equipped with sensitive items and high-frequency recording devices and with advertisements has very lame looking geniuses in the van. An agency in pursuit needs their database with high tech gadgets like a laptop connected directly to the mainframe of the CIA or Interpol, to evaluate any face in their database or to search for any information. This Web can record, broadcast the current feeds and upload them on to the database. The Web was a Mercedes-Benz Sprinter Cargo Van 3500 of light grey colour. From the outside, it could pass off as a frozen meat delivery van with advertisements on both sides, carrying pictures of deliciously cooked chicken or something and written 'Sainsbury's' with a tagline of 'Taste the delicacy'.

She joined the team on the ground with Matt, in case they needed a backup. She left the headquarters to reach Hero's square where Gopal was sitting on a bench for ten minutes and staring at the 19th century monuments.

A beautiful sculpture, one of its kind, but a nightmare for any surveillance team because of the crowd gathering to see the monuments. H'söktere (meaning 'Heroes' Square' in Hungarian) is surrounded by two important buildings – Museum of Fine Arts on the left and Hall of Art on the right. On the other side, it faced Andrássy Avenue which had two buildings overlooking the square – one residential and the other one the Embassy of Serbia. This place drew tourists from all over the world. It created a buzz all around and Madelyn thought she had made the right decision of bringing in the Web for surveillance because it was not humanly possible for anyone to hear anything or see anyone approaching and leaving Gopal at this place. Street artists and live performers had occupied this Heroes' Square. These were the physical challenges for her team to intercept any contact with Gopal, and the place had the Serbian embassy; a slight hint could trigger the alarm in the embassy. She assessed her options.

However, none of her suspicions were actually taking shape, and to her, that was disturbing. Then she overheard in one of her earpieces centrally connected to the Web, the CIA headquarters and the team on the ground watching Gopal, that her Web team had gotten into some situation with the local cops. Some cop found them suspicious enough to be parked there and forced them to come out of the vehicle. She commanded John to stay put and keep a close watch on Gopal while she handled the situation with the Web on her own. She pumped in all her energy to crunch the accelerator and broke all the traffic lights on her way to Heroes' Square. When she was busy cutting and skidding her car to full throttle, Matt made few calls to the local authorities to inform the police at

Hero's Square to stay put and not arrest any of their men. She was there in eight minutes. As soon as she hit the ground, she made her impact by flashing her badge. More importantly, the local policemen somehow got a call from every department head they knew and had been ordered to vanish from the scene. That's the impact CIA had on the Hungarian Embassy, or every agency for that matter. Once she gained control, she sat along with her geeky agents inside the Web and asked them to play the recordings, which they had missed. However, Gopal hadn't moved an inch according to the feeds captured by a high-frequency camera installed on the van. She was a little frustrated, but didn't show any sign to the others. She ordered them to keep a close watch on the guy and tasked another one to check every street performer, painter and anyone with a hood on his head. On her way back to her car parked nearby, she scanned every building around to see if she could get a glimpse of anyone over any building.

There was a time in the day around 3 p.m. when her suspicion was highly aroused seeing Gopal visiting the opera house in Budapest after having lunch with his son.

Budapest Opera House will enchant you not only with its ballet and opera performances, but also with its fine neo-Renaissance architecture – another outstanding opus of work from the 19th century. Afternoons did not have any opera show running, but still saw a lot of tourists with their tickets following many guides explaining, showing them the opera house.

It was about 3.30 p.m. when all of a sudden a bus stopped at the gate and a pile of people dressed as 17th-century people started coming in and merged with the group of people who were there for the tour, including CIA's target Gopal. They were there to rehearse their part in one of the best French opera acts named '*Orfeo Ed Euridice*'.

While the CIA was scanning every character, one of the geeks shouted by pointing his index to one of the monitors showing a live feed. Accompanied by Madelyn herself in the back of the Web, the geek showed her that a thin guy, with a black sweatshirt hoodie and a pair of shades just crossed camera 6 hurriedly. However, he was not spotted on camera 5, strangely because there was no way he could have skipped by the camera. This was sufficient for Madelyn to come to her conclusion that something was amiss. She was obviously convinced that Gopal was moving from one place to another on someone's instructions. So whoever was controlling Gopal's moves and making Madelyn frustrated had to contact Gopal physically, because Gopal did not have any call other than from his own son earlier. This could be the guy who could either be her actual target or accomplice. In any case, she had to catch the hooded guy. In a split second, she decided and spoke on her earpieces.

"Matt, you and I will cover the main entrance and will scan each of the individuals on our own. Dave, you will cover the back exit to see if someone tries to sneak out of there. Chuck, you and John get inside the opera from the back right now and check every goddamn inch of the building."

Her instructions were clear and the team of five men, including Madelyn, moved towards both the entry and exit points of the Opera House, leaving the two geeks still scanning the whole place through the CCTV cameras installed in the area. One of them was still scratching his head to understand how the hell the hooded guy managed to reach camera 6 without being seen at the exit and entry points. The other one was busy in clearing the distortions on the 2 second feed. However, the more he tried, the more he found that the hooded guy was too careful and there was no way they could even catch a glimpse of his face. All they captured was a guy with a hood and glasses on with blue trousers and sneakers. The guy was good, the geek thought, staring at the zoomed version. Suddenly his eyes lit up when the zoomed angle was able to capture a tattoo of some kind on the wrist of that man. He shouted on the earpiece to update the search party in the opera house that the guy had a tattoo on his right hand. It was hard to single out a person in this crowd where half of them were in their costumes and makeup on. But it was at least something which probably narrowed down the search a bit.

Madelyn responded, "Okay, send us his still on our mobiles and check if any information is available for this tattoo in our database."

Then Madelyn shifted her query to her partners in search of Matt, Chuck, and John.

"Anything from your end?"

Each one responded in the negative.

She then responded, "Keep looking, he can't just vanish."

Back in the Web, the geek captured the tattoo and started matching, the database centrally connected to the mainframe through the WAN connection. Suddenly a red flag error popped up, with an irritating tone. Some sort of virus threat!

No. The error said that a foreign device had been detected trying to breach the firewall settings on the router fixed inside the Web. The geeks looked at each other. Someone had tried to hack into their network. They started pounding the keys on their laptops, ran some prescripts and in seconds found the location of the foreign device. The location was showing a rather indigestible fact, that the foreign device was inside the Web. They looked at each other and one of the older ones spoke as if he found the root of the issue, "I told you to run maintenance on every single device last week. Did you do that?"

The other one shook his head.

"See now the router has blocked every access to our database, even us, you lazy ass!"

He showed his frustration and spoke again, "I am telling you, boy, I don't see your bright future here."

He started pounding the keyboard once again, as if he knew what to do next. The other one spoke softly, "Sorry, what are you doing now?"

"Nothing! I can't access the database now, so I have to reboot the router and see if I need the second router to take the primary path of connection."

The other one objected, "But it will shut down every camera and every device inside the Web."

He got an angry response from his senior still running some script on his computer, "I know dumb ass, it will hardly take twenty seconds to reboot, and besides that, I don't see any other option, do you?"

He was experienced enough, and it took exactly twenty seconds to reboot. The router started scanning the entire available device on the Web to connect back to the CIA database. It further took ten seconds and they were up again with the feeds and the database. The junior queried again, "What if someone tried to hack into us?"

Getting frustrated by seeing that their efforts of finding their target were failing, he did not like the idea of being judged by his irresponsible subordinate, so he exploded, "So you are saying that someone had tried to hack into the network which is invisible in this very Web, huh? Tell me, Mister. I can't see the third person with my naked eyes here"

And the senior geek got back to his database search for the tattoo symbol and murmured, "There is no foreign device; it was just a faulty router."

After twenty more seconds, the secondary router sent another warning message, but it was not fatal, so they ignored it. They had important work at hand. However, if they did look into it, they would have found out that it was just low-level information that the foreign device detected earlier had been encountered and neutralized. The messages followed by the MAC address of the foreign device. What that meant was that the foreign device was still inside the Web.

They were back on track and monitoring everything. Madelyn called off the search when Gopal left the opera at 4:17 p.m. and hired a taxi to visit the nearby town Szentendre. She ordered everyone to be prepared for and get access to every camera installed on the streets of Szentendre. She could not risk taking a chance to leave Gopal on the site, so her team followed him further. But she stayed at the opera house along with Matt for some more time to see if she could get hold of the hooded guy. However, it was as if the guy had vanished. She joined her team in a short while and followed Gopal until he reached the Indian embassy. She couldn't believe that she had nothing. There was definitely something missing.

She was lying back restless and staring at the ceiling of her air-conditioned not so tidy cabin, when she got a call on her Cisco IP phone. One of her analysts informed her that he had sent a transcript on her secure laptop, which he just intercepted, from one of the mobile phones at Mr Gopal Mahto's house, emphasizing further that she should pay attention to it. She listened to the transcript twice and called Matt Oscar into her room. Matt arrived to find her standing near the wooden wall, back facing and with a cigarette, staring at the large map of Budapest covered with notes. She was in her black suit with the same coloured skirt, and black transparent leggings, He saw her high heels lying on the other side of the room. Those heels would make anyone uncomfortable in one hour, but that was Madelyn for you. That was her statement, a very hard and a bold one. She had been married twice, but both her husbands couldn't keep up with her obsession and determination towards her duty. Since then she had understood that marriage was not her thing. She was broken inside with the divorce; after all, she was deeply in love with him. She had had a tough childhood with her abusive father and mother. She had always been a punching bag of a drunk and impotent father and sometimes-frustrated mother having extramarital affairs. Madelyn had always felt insecure as a child. Therefore, when she grew up, she found a way to channelize her insecurity and found great pleasure securing her own country. This was something most common with every spy – an unhappy childhood.

Matt had always been her closest and profound follower in the department, and Madelyn knew it very well.

"Matt, there is a transcript which our OPS team has just intercepted. It looks like our ally has still not understood the fact that their strange actions will only demolish their credibility... not only with the US, but also with NATO. Such fools... huh?"

She had always been commanding in her tone.

"Look what we have found, the Indian first secretary is bringing some lunatic of their agency RAW to hit... us here... again?"

After a long time she finished her cigarette, which was by now half burnt. Matt's response was as if she had cracked a joke,

"Yes... right..."

But when he saw her sucking her cigarette inactively with an emotionless face, he understood how serious she was.

"You mean they are planning to hit us... the CIA... here in Budapest? No, no they have been a good friend to us, how can they think of doing this?"

She spoke judgmentally, "I am not sure what's on their mind, but Gopal used his son's phone and contacted three different sources to get three different things – one was the report filed by local police of the assassination of our own agents, the second was a map of a building, and the third was a forger. Our analyst found out that the building is ours, the exact same building we are in right now."

Matt was clearly speechless, so Madelyn continued, "Whoever is looking to break into our house, he will try and get a forged ID. So I want you to change every single one of our staff's ID's access code right away. This includes you and me. Next, you install a new power source and switch our security cameras to that source, be mindful of using our own engineer to do that within the next five hours."

She saw Matt was obedient enough to make notes on his palm device but interrupted her, "But how do we know when we are going to get a hit?"

"As of now even I don't have any idea, but as Gopal demanded over the phone he needed all the information by tonight, so my best guess would be tomorrow post lunch."

Before Matt could speak, he saw her jaws clench visibly in anger. "You know what, I want this bastard to get inside our house and I swear to god, I will bury him with my bare hands!"

Then she started to give a chain of instructions to secure the building, while Matt noted down. The meeting went on for almost an hour before Matt stepped out, leaving her in the exact same situation, when he came in, carefully watching the map of Budapest with her fifth burnt cigarette.

Her frustration was not only with her failure to catch the actual assassin, but also not being able to trace him until then. She now knew that the bus driver identified as Sijo Varghese was code-named 'Virat'. If she nailed this guy while trying to breach CIA's den, she would be able to gain her reputation in the eyes of Hamilton. Then Hamilton would screw RAW the way he wanted to in an international court, with proper evidence.

Twelve

The Red, Escape

23rd September
Miles away

While Madelyn was busy formulating the plan to grab Arya, he reached his current hideout in Budapest. As soon as he opened the door, Aisha came rushing towards him with worried eyes,

"Did everything go well? Where were you all this time? I was so worried since you asked me to head back here from the Opera House!"

"You are being childish, Miss Bahar."

Arya's words were like a medicine to her, she pressed her lips to his for a while. Then she stopped kissing and, hugged him tight. She spoke in a coquettish way, "You are a spy, I am not. I can't handle the pressure of not knowing where you have been all this while."

Arya and Aisha were falling for each other since their stay in the apartment back in Turkey. Two lonely souls on the run, dodging every threat that could end their life, tended to find comfort in each other. Arya detached himself from her tight embrace, and fixed his eyes on hers, "I am done with this shit."

She couldn't believe his words.

Arya spoke again, "I am sorry for today, that this bloody job made me use you as bait too." Arya was clearly feeling guilty.

She giggled and responded by tugging his chin up, "Ah! I don't care for my life anymore. I am okay to be used as long as I… can… use what I love the most!"

She paused frequently between her words and her eyes had a sparkle with a lusty smile. "And what would that be?" Arya had almost the same posture as hers. She slid her hands through his jacket and T-shirt to reach and feel him. She licked and kissed his chest through his V-shaped woollen T-shirt and showed her desire. Arya laughed and said,

"Aisha stop it… we don't have time for this… we are leaving!"

She stopped herself at once, rolled her eyes and tried to figure out what she had just heard. She did manage to hide her anxiety from Arya though. She was still holding him, but her grip loosened. She asked after a while with a flat tone, "You got what you wanted?"

"I will tell you on the way back, please hurry up."

A sudden chill descended in the room as she went back to the bathroom and closed the door behind. She returned, dressed in a woollen high-neck pullover, black jeans with boots, and a shiny black leather jacket. She saw a man, standing in the living area, who at first was unrecognizable. She then realized it was Arya. She never expected Arya to transform himself in this way. She fixed her gaze on him. He had trimmed his hair short, bleached his beard and a few parts of his hair evenly. His fair complexion suited this half-bald look perfectly. He also used coloured contact lenses. A Jewish cap, known as the kippah, was at the centre of his head. He was standing and looking at himself in the mirror. She gradually reached up to him, when he turned there were thick glasses over his eyes. He looked like an ethnic Jew, aged around thirty. The thick glasses fixed on his face made him look like a schoolteacher. Jews were found in every part of the world, especially in Europe. It was a perfect cover for Arya at the Hungarian-Austrian border.

"Look what they made us give up," Arya was showing his first sign of frustration.

After giving each other knowing looks, he changed the topic and handed over a small jewellery box, "This thing made me late today!"

Aisha opened it. It was a nose pin. She replaced it with the older one she was wearing and tried every angle to see how this small, beautiful piece of ornament looked on her face. It was a stunning piece of jewellery, which made her look more elegant! It suited her fair face perfectly. "You impress me repeatedly! Your return gift will satisfy you, when we stop next. By the way, you forgot to tell me about where we are headed now?"

He opened the door and checked the surroundings before responding, "Vienna."

Hungarian-Austrian Border checkpoint
Hegyeshalom Village
10 p.m.

The Border Security personnel dressed in the National Guard uniform signalled the next car in the queue to come and park near his booth for a formal check as he let the couple enter Vienna. Once they were through the checkpoint, Arya reclined his seat and closed his eyes. During the course of these two hours, she felt like asking him more than once about why he had suddenly changed his plan. As far as she suspected, he had taken the risk to come into Budapest to understand and grab sufficient Intel that could prove his employer's innocence in the assassination of the three Americans along with Mir and three Iranian nationals a week ago. She was happy knowing that her sadist ex Mir was dead. That rapist got what he deserved – a bullet in between his eyes.

Vienna – 'the city of music'. It had the same feel as Budapest. The two cities, (Budapest and Vienna) were like twin sisters. Both cities shared the same Danube river only spelt differently as Donau in Vienna. It divided Vienna exactly the same way it did Budapest. The weather was not so pleasant outside, with snow on the streets and a chill in the air. It was windy too; people from the South Asian region were bound to feel it in their bones. The only visible difference between Budapest and Vienna is the language. In Vienna, people used German as their primary language, but had a fair bit of understanding of English as well. The hotel was a two star one but looked comfortable enough for the night. It was around midnight and they both badly needed to rest.

What bothered her most was that when they were running all day, only to find out who's following who, how did Arya manage to get the information he needed? On the other hand, she was convinced that this guy would have never left Budapest until he had found out what the real story was; but what was it? Only he knew. He used a credit card with the name of Abraham Hazzan at the reception. Thanks to Razeeq for arranging all the fake IDs and required papers, along with a credit card with some real money.

◆

Gopal Mahato only knew that a RAW agent would make a contact. Arya reached Budapest on 21st September, two days prior to sniffing out how Gopal was reacting and whether or not showing any signs of breakdown. His whole purpose would fail if Gopal ditched RAW's offer for help. Arya was restless and ran around day and night discreetly; it was not at all a one-man job. The job required to be in more than two places at every second, and that was the same reason Arya couldn't refuse her offer to help him in this short, hostile endeavour.

Yesterday, Arya made sure that Gopal's pursuers clicked so many pictures of unidentified men he had made Gopal sit with, laugh with, and talk with during the day trip. The CIA must have been broken down to their core searching every person in their database, but the man they intended to find was never in front of them. He was perpetually behind them. By the first half of the day, Arya was sure that the tailing was done by two different vehicles – first the sedan Alfa Romeo 159 with three passengers. A woman in her casuals did the second. An African-American in an Audi along with the other ethnic American male; her looks, and her posture made him certain that she was senior case officer. Arya found out later that her name was Madelyn Hunter.

During all these times, Arya chose a nearby high building with a good vantage point. He sat on the rooftop with tiny palm-sized binoculars to see if his plan was making progress with the exact pace and precise timing that he had calculated.

Arya made sure that the CIA's tail team got tired and vulnerable, and most importantly, he got them adjusted to the idea that the man they were pursuing was not doing anything out of the unusual. The key was to find a blind spot to let himself in and be near his target – the Web. Arya had to keep in mind that the people he was planning to play with during the operation were easily disposable and had no evidence linking it back to him. He fed them with money or sometimes with his interpersonal skills to convert them to his assets on the field. He only wanted them to play a particular character on a big real life stage, keeping in mind that every character just knows what he has to do; nobody can see the big picture at any stage, that's called deception. This was the deception of a spy, who was getting furious, smart, and smooth day by day, minute by minute, second by second.

When she returned in her red nightgown, she was struck by the cold breeze like a dagger. Someone had opened the balcony door at 1 a.m. Must be Arya, she thought. She ran and grabbed something warmer to feel comfortable and let herself out into the balcony. It was dark outside, and the first thing she noticed was a half-filled glass with a black liquid, which looked like rum and a freshly burnt cigarette stub lying on the balcony's edge. There was Arya sitting on a stool outside, staring at the limitless city of Vienna.

"What are you doing? Come inside, you will catch a cold."

A protective concern that Arya chose to ignore.

She repeated herself. This time Arya responded in exasperation, "Will you please shut up? And stop behaving like a wife!"

"Why you are behaving like a dick? I am not trying to be your wife, nor do I have any urge of being treated like your whore!"

She rushed out of the balcony and into the room and started packing whatever she had unpacked in a hurry.

Arya went and grabbed her from behind without her permission. She had those little tears in her eyes again.

Arya admitted, "I am a dick head! And you are right, I am sorry. Forgive me!"

She pushed him away forcefully and moved towards the door to walk out of the room to stay alone. All she wanted was to not see his face again; she was very furious and wished to walk out barefooted. She felt humiliated for trusting a man again. She was not at all in the mood to understand him, and why should she? After all, she had nothing to gain being with him. She could have chosen to be at any place, anywhere safe from all this spy shit, but instead, she trusted him and tried to be his genuine partner. Before she could open the door and let herself out, Arya grabbed her and drew her closer, and before she knew it, he pressed his lips on hers.

She tried to push him away, but he didn't let her go easily. There was no way she would let him use her again. She began hitting him rapidly on his chest and his face with her fist. But he didn't let her go any more than an inch of him, his lips were still on hers. She hated the fact that she was losing it and tried one last time to free her lips by biting him. It worked; he let go of her briefly. She saw a pinch of blood on his rims. Her hair dishevelled, she looked like an angry, wild kitten. Arya again reached out to her and grabbed her by the waist, only to lift her a little above the ground. She didn't resist him; her hatred was by now all gone. The chilly wind ensured the fact that both of them felt passionate enough to kiss again. She grabbed him and wrapped her legs around his waist. She felt being forced against the rampart. But she didn't object to his rough approach, nor did he look like he cared for her objections. Their playfulness continued from the wall to the study desk, where out of passion, she kicked the night lamp. The lamp fell to the floor and shattered, with the glass strewn all over. The frenzy continued on the floor and ended with both sides submitting. Roughly, about twenty minutes later, they were both exhausted but satisfied. At that moment, they felt the cold freeze their blood. Just in time, Arya managed to close the balcony door and grab his leftover rum from the edge.

He came back to the room and found his partner shivering under the blanket. He offered her the rest of the drink in his glass; she gulped it without a second thought. It left a burning sensation within her. He lit up a cigarette and joined her under the blanket. She was shaking all over due to cold, so she snuggled deep into the blanket and held him tightly.

After a good five minutes or so, she poked out her head, and said, "We should do this frequently, don't you think? Can I have a puff?" He passed her the packet.

"Will you now tell me why you shouted at me?" she broke the silence.

Arya took out his phone, and showed her the files. These files had CIA stuff in it. The report was brief and had details about the assassination – the key evidence found on the body of every dead man on the bus, the toxic element, which made them paralyzed before the 9 mm bullet passed through their skull. It also had details about how the assassin's dead body was recovered from the river. It had their fingerprints, pictures, and short bios. Arya confirmed that it was, in fact, his team who killed all the men.

She inquired, "It can be doctored, but how did you manage to get the CIA files? Who gave them to you?"

He responded 'CIA', she responded, "Ha-ha... did they hand over the files to you? Personally? Seriously, who's your source?"

"I am not kidding, I hacked into their system, and downloaded them all," Arya said with a flat face.

"Wait... What? When? How?" She became fully alert and rose from his chest.

"It doesn't matter. What matters is my team did this and now I have evidence." Her gaze dropped in disappointment. However, she insisted he tell her.

"Alright..." Arya resumed with a momentary pause, "I did it when we were at the opera house, and I asked you to come out of that direction with your hood on. I wanted every field agent to run for you, leaving the nerds back in the van. When I saw it had created enough chaos in their minds, I remotely activated the device just to try and get it self-connected to the router placed under the Web."

"Device? Which device?"

"When I asked you to call the cops and inform them about a suspicious van standing at Heroes' Square."

"Yes, and then the cops tried to arrest people inside the van... and then you might have got some distraction to place your device inside it... got it... then what?"

"When my device tried to connect to their network, their router forced every other device out of its zoned network. In such a case, every device is left wondering, sending its Wi-Fi signals to any available connection while leaving its trace, which is known as the MAC address. Every device has its own unique code of numbers, but since it's all CIA's gadgets, so it had a unique sequence not found on ordinary devices such as a laptop, palm devices or mobile phones. Which I easily got just by offering my WI-FI network signal! Of course, they will not connect since my router is again a foreign device for them, but my purpose was served as I managed to get the same sequence of the MAC addresses as the CIA's. I then masked the same MAC address to my device under the van, which then pretended to be one of the CIA's own gadgets to the router, before one of the nerds in the van had rebooted it. Therefore, when the CIA router searched its zoned device, my device was available for a connection or let's just say I was able to shortly violate the network protocols for some seconds. I was counting for thirty seconds, but it kicked me out at twenty-seven and that is how I was connected to their mainframe. Their own router let me walk in to their mainframe and I collected the information I needed before the router actually found out about the device as an outsider and dismantled it. CIA routers have such a highly sophisticated program, it not only prevents hacking but also damages any foreign device."

When he stopped, she was half-asleep. She had a cheerful laugh when she saw Arya's face. He couldn't believe that he was so seriously telling her a nail-biting, mind-boggling tale of hacking the CIA and she had just yawned. She fought hard to keep her eyes open, but showed him that she was still interested in knowing what happened next as he scrolled down to the last part of the report. He then started summarizing further different, but relevant reports to her.

It seemed Farooq, one other team member, was caught by the CIA. The file showed that the moment he was captured, an elite group of expert interrogators flew in and took him away. By doing so, they made their intentions clear that they did not trust even their local resources in Budapest to lead the interrogation, which was Madelyn Hunter.

"The CIA is keeping him in a safe house facility in Frankfurt called '*Großstadt*' located downtown. This file was updated yesterday just before I got it; it seems that Farooq is somehow holding up and hasn't broken down yet."

"They will break him eventually, I am afraid."

"I have to get him out. I can't let them use him against RAW… no… I need to kill him," Arya didn't know what he was talking about evidently.

"Or get killed, is that what you want? Till now, whatever you have done was up to a limit and you had an advantage of not been actually seen by anyone, but this is suicidal. No, no, no… I won't let you die by some childish urge of being a hero, and for what, whom? Huh… It is clear that… the people from your own side have betrayed you and have put your existence within questionable brackets. How can you be so dumb to not see that?"

She was frustrated with his approach towards the situation, so she threw many questions at him. There was silence in the room before again she spoke with a protective tone.

"Look, I understand you have not lived a single day without a purpose, a purpose that supersedes everything. Even your life… and that purpose is to defend your motherland. I am not saying you shouldn't do that….."

She saw no reaction from him.

"Are you listening to what I am saying? I will not let you ruin yourself. I will not let you ruin us… or have you decided to let me shout at you all night?"

He responded, "Let's not talk about it now. Please…"

There was no point in arguing with a woman.

"You got the proof. Pass this message to your superiors back home and let them deal with it." She cupped his face with her palm, and spoke while fixing her gaze on him. It's a perfect way out. Nobody knows you are here, we can vanish and live somewhere quietly."

He was silent; she made perfect sense. His own ideology didn't matter now, Virat did kill everyone. With or without the consent of RAW, but if anyone had to be blamed for this, it was RAW. They chose that crooked bastard to lead this mission, which led to the disgrace of the whole nation.

She was irritated with his silence and shouted, "Why don't you say something?"

"It's not a decision I can make on the fly."

He felt strange every time he got close to this beautiful creature; he was haunted by Shubhendu's words in his memory. Shubhendu always said to the recruits that getting into a relationship was quite normal; you are allowed to do that. It makes your cover perfect. However, being attached to someone in a relationship is what you are not allowed; it clouds your judgment. Arya felt he was hanging on a broken barbwire in the valley of death and love.

She was sleeping calmly and had not changed her position since the last few hours. He was sitting near her, witnessing her beauty. It was about three o'clock in the morning; there was a mild but steady snowfall and it was still dark and feathery outside. He kissed her, gently on her forehead for a brief moment, and then left the room. He needed to clear his head, so he decided to go for a stroll. He didn't even care to dress up enough for the freezing godforsaken weather.

Thirteen

The Red, Hunt

Arya crossed the road and came to a narrow alley joining the main road from both ends. As he approached from the other side of the alley where a few cars were parked, a Land Rover entered the alley from the right end. Jet-black in colour, it was heading towards him slowly. He stood in front of an old Fiat and pretended to be searching for the keys. Arya acted as if he had dropped the keys on the ground and sat down to find it, as the car passed by him smoothly and quietly. Arya was sure that none of the two men inside the Land Rover had spotted him. They might be some ordinary people. Nevertheless, he couldn't be sure, so he chose to hide behind the Fiat. Then he overheard the conversation between the people in the Land Rover in a language he was well rehearsed with. It made his heart skip a beat,

"Shit!" Not them… it cannot be!"

Without thinking much, he pressed the remote button on the key, which unlocked a car at a distance with a beep. One of the items he had pickpocketed earlier from one of the hotel guests before getting inside the hotel room; he wanted to discard the car he drove from Budapest. The beep made Arya realize that the car was a few yards away from his current hideout. He hurried towards the car, ducking his head, and opened the car door to get in. Well before he could enter, a bullet came rushing towards him and passed through his right arm, making a neat exit from the other side.

The jolt of the bullet pushed him rolling towards the adjacent wall. These foreign agents were here to shoot him down. One thing was clear – "Shoot to wound, but not to kill". He felt an immense pain and a shriek came out of his mouth. The gun the bullet came from surely had a silencer, and belonged to one of the guys who was in the passenger seat and was now standing near the Land Rover, which by now was blocking Arya's exit to the main road. The same skull-faced foreigner also fired a second and a third shot at him simultaneously in quick succession, but Arya managed to dodge them and got into the car. The artistic design of the interiors of the car assured him that it was the Jaguar XKR convertible, Piano Black. In normal circumstances, he would have enjoyed the ride, but... tonight was not one of his days. He felt lucky though that the Jaguar's back was facing the Land Rover. He just needed to drive straight and survive those bloody shots hitting the car from the back. He had to reach the other side of the alley, the back side of the luxury hotel. He sprang over to the driver's side, pressed the electric switch and wrenched it into first gear as the engine exploded into life. Arya released the hand brake and the car leaped forward. He pressed his foot down on the accelerator and headed straight to the other side of the alley. It was just a matter of ten seconds, and he would have passed the alley and those gunshots. He was not lucky this time, as out of the blue, a bin lorry entered the alley and stopped immediately. Arya squeezed the hand brake and the Jaguar stopped immediately. One of the shooters hit the lorry as well. The driver of lorry ran off, leaving the lorry parked mid-way in the alley, which blocked Arya's escape route, and probably his only chance of survival. The Jaguar was continuously hammered down with bullets fired by those two genius foreigners. The only other path out was the other side of the alleyway, which was occupied by the Land Rover. There was no time to think.

He released the hand brake and moved to the reverse gear, pressed his foot down on the accelerator, and headed towards the Land Rover in reverse. This bold move shocked the foreigners, but one of them jumped into the Land Rover and tried to dash into the Jaguar from the back. The other man was shooting at him, constantly. Arya slid down in his seat a bit to save himself, and continuously checked the small monitor fixed inside the Jaguar that showed him the path backwards. It was just a matter of seconds before there could be a collision in the alley between these two beasts – the Jaguar and his opponent, the Land Rover.

There was a huge roaring sound in the alley as the two beasts dared each other to get out of the way. Before the Land Rover could dash into the Jaguar, Arya swung the steering 360 degrees to the right and before kissing the front of the Rover, he swung it back around 180 degrees. Anyone who witnessed that would have agreed that it was exemplary. With a fluent move with the steering wheel, the Jaguar made a snake turn. All though there was not much space left in between the Land Rover and alley wall, the Jaguar managed to sneak past the Rover. The Jaguar thrashed the rear-view mirror of the Land Rover before running free towards the end of the alley. Sparks flew up into the air.

Arya, who had nearly reached the end of the alley by now and had to merge with the running traffic on the main road. He pressed hard on the brakes and turned his wheels to its full again; the Jaguar did the rest. This animal made a broad statement on the running traffic, as many cars stopped immediately and crashed into each other at the back. Arya skid ahead into the main road. The back of the Jaguar was still unsteady; he steered the wheel and pressed the accelerator just enough to regain control. Once he had straightened up, he changed gear and roared off. He headed straight, hoping to get away from the place and hide out somewhere until it was safe. He was soon on the outskirts of the town and was feeling quite pleased with himself when he saw the dark bulk of a car pulling up alongside. He quickly turned his head to see the Land Rover, with the same skull-faced man at the wheel, and the younger man at his side.

Hell! It wasn't quite over yet!

Arya dropped into a lower gear and stomped the pedal. The engine didn't complain and speeded up. After a second, with the revs almost off the dial, he changed up, then up again. The Jaguar was flat out now, going more than a hundred miles an hour.

He kept his speed up, but was blinded by the sweat that was pouring into his eyes. He wiped his face and saw that he was in the open countryside. Out of town, there were no streetlights and all he could see clearly was the small patch of brightness that his headlamps made in front of him.

A mixture of panic, fear and impatience to get back to the hotel, gripped Arya. To get an answer. He could feel his body shaking and rattling. Every tiny bump on the road felt like he was hitting a great boulder. His face froze, his lips forced back from his aching teeth with anger. He fought to keep the car under control as it bounced over the road.

He didn't know if he could outrun the Land Rover. It was larger and heavier than the Jaguar, and, the skull-faced man had the advantage of being able to follow Arya's taillights. Arya had nothing.

He was just about to look around to see how far behind the Land Rover was when he felt a mighty jolt and heard a bang.

They had rammed into him. He swerved across the road and narrowly avoided hitting a car going the other way, shrouded in a spray of ice. He fought to get the Jaguar back under his control and coaxed a little more speed out of the beast. The collision had not caused any serious damage, but if they rammed again, he might not be so lucky, looking at his condition with a wounded right hand and the immense pain.

He thought of shooting back at them, but as soon as he picked his piece, he knew it had an empty chamber. It was lighter than the last time he checked. He clenched his teeth and shouted, "Bitch!"

There were lights up ahead and they thundered into a village. This was the village of Grinzing in Vienna with a brief blur of houses and a tomb and then darkness up ahead, flat and featureless for miles around. There was no place to hide out; it was totally exposed. Arya wasn't sure how long he could keep it up. He was driving on instinct; the thinking part of his brain was shutting down. His eyes were stinging, and no matter how often he blinked them, he could barely see anything. Then he saw the glove box. He leaned over and fumbled to find something to help his condition. There was a small Coke tin, his fingers closed around the cane strap and he yanked it out. He spilled most over his face and on his injured hand, one by one. For a moment, he almost instantly blinded by the pain as the soda hit his wounds like a dagger, but then the bubbles and coke were on his face and he felt a spark in his loosening senses. He drank the rest of it and felt good almost instantly. He had to wipe his face clean, and hold on to the steering wheel tightly. Then he shouted out loudly, "Come on, you motherfuckers!"

Once again, the Land Rover rammed him from behind and his head jerked painfully back. If they keep up this crazy chase, they would eventually run out of either road or crash. Either way, being captured was inevitable. After all, they were Ukrainian mercenaries. How did he know it? The weapon used by them – the Glock 18 fully automatic. A very peculiar type of asshole in his business. They knew him and said the exact words, "He is the target!"

In the next village, they came too close, but Arya suddenly took a right fork and left the main road. Then he took a series of wild turns and switchbacks in an effort to shake off the Land Rover. At every turn, however, the Land Rover kept up with him. Twice it pulled alongside and tried to nudge him off the road and it was only by wrenching the wheel and manoeuvring the car with all his strength that Arya held the tarmac.

At last, in the small district of Tulln, he saw his chance. A broken-down lorry blocked the icy road. There was a gap just wide enough to squeeze the Jaguar through, but there was no way the Land Rover could follow.

Arya threw the car into the opening. There was a hideous scraping and screeching as he ground against the lorry. Sparks flew. He glanced back. There was no sign of the Land Rover. He shouted in triumph.

He'd made it.

Just.

He was exhausted. He was out of options, driving in a daze, not sure where he was going or what he should do next. The shock of finding that Aisha ditched him wasn't enough. However, she surely saw to it that he would never survive. She bloody sold him to them for what? Why?

She couldn't do that. She didn't have it in her. Or maybe it was Razeeq? He was convinced in his heart. He could have leaked the credit card information. He was a bloody smuggler, after all. However, if he did it, they would have captured him at the border itself.

It could only be her, 'the bitch!'

Driving at full speed, with all that shit in his head about her all the time had drained him. He struggled to keep his eyes open and remain focused. When he thought about what she'd just done, he didn't know whether to laugh or to cry. He had been too faithful to her, his honey trapper. Why would she endanger herself all along, coming to Budapest with him, and selling him out at Vienna? Who was her real master?

He wiped his face for the hundredth time and the blood turned to ice in his veins and in his injured arm.

How could he be so fooled, he gutted himself? The way she carried his instructions at the opera house, even the CIA couldn't catch her as the hooded man.

He peered ahead. He would recognize the pattern of those twin beams anywhere. They were burnt into his brain. It was the Land Rover again. It had stopped in the middle of the road. Somehow, they had come around him and ahead.

"Oh... Fuck me!"

She had placed a tracker on him, he was now sure.

Sickened to the core, the very next second, he thought, "Well, damn them. Damn those two assholes to hell. If these two are the furious mercenaries, then to give them hell, here he is, he is RAW!"

He pushed the accelerator down and aimed straight at them.

He wasn't thinking about anything; he was just staring at the lights as they got bigger and bigger. He would drive straight between them, if necessary.

He cackled.

It had finally happened. He'd gone crazy. Love can make you blind, and betrayal can make you wild.

He saw the panicked faces of the two men as he reached closer.

"Come on, assholes!" said Arya, through clenched teeth. "Come, die with me!"

At the last moment, the skull-faced man decided that he was going to get out of the way.

In a mad scramble, he juddered off the road into an icy ditch. Arya shot past him, whooping in triumph, but then his eyes stretched wide in horror. The Land Rover had been blocking his view of the road ahead. There was a stiff turn ahead. Moreover, if he couldn't manage to take this turn, there was a cliff of rocks about twenty feet high and a small channel of the Danube River flowing below with high current. Arya turned his steering wheel in a flash, but that was his first mistake, probably last. With the sudden turn in the front wheels at this speed, the wheels lost contact with the ground, and flipped the Jaguar upside down. It started bouncing like a cricket ball. The front of the car crunched as it bottomed into the slope and Arya was thrown forward! He was about to smash his face against the steering wheel, but was saved by the airbags. Still holding the wheel, Arya flew through space. The nose of the car dropped and it performed a lazy somersault. He was aware of the ground rushing by and flipping over, then he was thrown clear, not knowing which way was up or down. He soon found out, though, when he flipped out of the open door and thudded into a bed of weeds at the river's edge. He was jarred and winded, and for a split second, he blacked out. Then he heard a great thump for the last time as the car hit the riverbank some twenty feet ahead. A great spray of water exploded when the Jaguar finally sank into the river below. The displaced water drenched him and made him stick to the bed of weeds at the river's edge.

He struggled groggily to his feet and hauled himself up to the bank, his feet sinking into the thick wet sludge. The car was resting upside down. Befuddled and confused, Arya staggered forward. He had not even gone three steps that he flung backward at least six feet, as the petrol in the car's tank exploded.

He was unconscious before he hit the edge of the river.

When he came to his senses, he found himself alone by the river's edge. Where were those two scumbags? Probably they saw only the explosion and not Arya flipping out of the car. They must be coming down here to search the exploded car. He would not try to outrun them; he would finish them.

One of them was swift and came rushing down in a few minutes. Arya certainly saw his chance. The night was too dark to have a clear visibility around and they didn't know that Arya was alive. Arya wasn't holding any weapon to tackle the first one coming near the Jaguar. The bitch had emptied his gun, it was unfair. He only needed one shot, but how could he… maybe if he had a knife or some sort of sharp object.

"Ah!" a shriek almost came out of his throat, but he managed to bear the pain he felt in the left side of his abdomen. There was a piece of glass stuck in his abdomen. When the Jaguar exploded, the shattered glass must have got embedded in his body. It was a rather large piece of glass with a sharp edge. He had found his weapon of choice. He gathered himself and pulled it out amidst immense pain. He chose to lie low on the muddy part of the river and moved towards the burning car. The younger man had reached the Jaguar and was trying to see if there was anybody inside through the small flames. He turned and spoke to the skull-faced man who was coming down to the scene, "That bastard is not here!"

The skull-faced man replied, "He must be there, look again!" and for a moment he looked down to watch his step again. The young man found Arya this time, but not dead. Standing right in front of him covered in mud, eyes bloody red. The younger man quickly reached for his gun, and at the same time, Arya swung the sharp-edged glass through his left hand. It wasn't about who pulled the weapon first; it was a matter of who wanted to survive in this business. Clearly, Arya was the one who had thrust enough to survive again. Arya made a wild cut on the throat of the young man before he could pull the trigger and his enemy was on his knees. Arya didn't watch him die, but rather got hold of his gun and fired a deadly shot at the skull-faced man, who was still struggling to get down to the scene. The bullet penetrated the man's skull, and the old Ukrainian sank to the muddy shore.

He searched the younger one first. There was nothing much, but he was surely a Ukrainian, as their accent suggested. His head spun for a second, not only because of the injuries and blood loss, but a deadly thought of her.

Arya swiftly discarded his own clothes, sim card, wallet, and everything in his possession at the river, and got into the clothes of the young man. If she had something on him, some sort of a tracker, he'd be safe now. He wanted to kick himself, for being such an obvious fool.

How can I be such a dumb fuck? She was always a turncoat, he thought, but on the other hand, he needed someone to get into Budapest, form a trap, execute his plan and get out alive before the CIA even got wind of him. It was one man versus the CIA if he assessed his choices. It was he who needed her more than she needed him.

After seventy miles or so in his assailants' Land Rover, Arya heard the GPS guiding him to the Vienna International Airport. He realised this was the same route taken by them to get out of Budapest a few hours ago. At the same time, a thought hit him. His face was determined, his eyes narrowed and he murmured, "Why does an eyes only file have a clear

location of Farooq's whereabouts? Who does that? We don't!
How come the CIA...."

He turned the wheel in a different direction. He neither
took the straight route to Budapest nor went to the airport. Was
he not supposed to reach Frankfurt to get Farooq out of CIA's
possession and question him by himself? Or he guessed Farooq
is not there as per CIA files. However, one thing was clear to
him – the path he had chosen would not be approved by anyone
with their head in its right place. It was suicidal to even think
of hitting a CIA safe house alone, especially when they were
protecting a high-value target of an assassination. They must
be armed to their teeth. Seeking for any help would clearly
jeopardize his intention; he chose to walk alone on this path. He
was certain that if he did go back to the hotel, his love interest
wouldn't be there.

Fourteen

The Red, Successors

Rotherham City, Yorkshire
1991

Anaya was on a break from her day job at an open café. Lunchtime was over and there was a good one hour left before people came in again for evening snacks. The wind was getting warmer and heralding the arrival of summer in the city, sooner than anticipated. For seating in this cafe, two chairs were placed with a table in between and there were five such sets. They were placed on the pavement and Anaya was sitting on a chair there, with a coffee mug on the table. In her free time, she liked reading the newspaper, which she picked up every day from a bookstore while coming to work.

A man approached her, crossing the quiet boulevard. The man gave her a sealed envelope and left quietly. Her suspicion turned positive when she opened that envelope. She rose from her seat, went inside the café and told her colleagues, 'Please tell Grimes that I am not coming to work anymore!'

◆

Itanagar, India
A week after

A young girl in a journalist's attire walked up to the farmhouse twenty kilometres away from the main city limits of Itanagar. She chose to complete the last ten by foot because out of this distance, five didn't have a decent road. There were a few huts around this old farm, and the nearest one was a thousand yards down this green hill. She reached the wooden four feet square gate of the farm by noon, which she hesitated to open. She briefly scanned the place first; there were quite a lot of local villagers seated in the garden area. This small group was a mix of men, women and children. Men and women were busy making handicrafts, and the children were at play. There was a huge blackboard at the corner, which was proof that these villagers were getting educated with an opportunity to earn some money as well. It all looked like an NGO.

Anaya knew that Reema had passed away, but before her death, she made all the necessary arrangements for her worthless son to survive in this world. She used her contacts with RAW and created this non-profit NGO named the Tegi Welfare Society. This place fell in a restricted zone because it was a border area, which was inhabited by tribal people, so it needed a special permit – the Inner Line Permit – usually issued by the Ministry of Home Affairs. Reema probably knew very well that her son would blow away all of their fortunes, so she formed this group so that at least regular funds reach in the name of this NGO and be sufficient for Mannu to survive.

A woman in a pleated sari approached Anaya at the gate and enquired about the purpose of her visit.

"I am here to see Moolchand sir," Anaya spoke in Hindi.

The woman had a very cold approach; an empty heart can easily spot another empty one.

"Come inside," she led the way inside the farmhouse by letting Anaya in by opening that jammed wooden gate. Her Hindi was rusty because of her tribal roots.

She directed Anaya to the left corner of that two-storey wooden vintage villa, where a man was seated in his wooden chair. He was taking a nap in this breezy weather under the occasional bright sun. When she reached near him, she found a plate with stains of rice and *daal* and vegetable curry on it. He was in his late forties and looked overweight with a bulky face and creepy eyes. For her, he would always be the pig and now her target, Mannu. She felt an irresistible urge just to bite off his throat with her bare teeth. This pig could be slaughtered anytime she wanted to, and she knew killing him softly would only satisfy her. Instead, she wanted to enjoy every moment of his last days, which by the way had just begun.

She tapped his shoulder. He came to his full attention. Mannu knew that a girl named Anaya was coming to meet him, but never knew she would be such a beautiful creature. He shouted for someone to come, clean the table, and bring some tea for the guest. The same woman came out.

Anaya showed him enough fake papers to prove to him that she was a correspondent of an international news channel and was tasked to cover a story on Indian tribes. Since his NGO had a reach to almost all of these tribes, it would be easy for her to achieve the goal. He looked convinced, but not interested, neither to help nor at her womanhood. At the same time, one of the young tribal girls came near them, out of curiosity to see her camera. Anaya clearly observed Mannu, and saw a sudden dramatic change in his eyes. He picked up the girl in his arms and asked if she wanted some chocolate. The girl agreed. He then excused himself and went inside the villa. To her knowledge, Mannu was now a widower; his wife never had a child and had died early. The reasons for him not getting married again became clear to her when he came back; his interest lay in a very different genre. He had satisfied glum look on his face, and the stains on his pyjama confirmed that he was still a bastard. For him, this NGO gave him enough resources for his sick pleasure. However, Mannu did give her the permission to work and do whatever she needed to.

From then on, she became a frequent visitor to the place, taking lots of pictures and recording stories.

After a year, a full-page article on the tenth page of a local English newspaper *Arunachal Front* covered a story on the work done by NGOs in helping local tribes in the Northeastern states. In the cover story, a substantial amount of attention was given to the Tegi Welfare Society, looking at the contribution made by this non-profit society for the past nine months. Rituparna Davidar, the spokesperson, expressed in general how a non-governmental organization could play a vital role in the progress of a state, especially when the government is neglecting the masses. Anaya read it for the third time since the newspaper was delivered this morning at the villa. However, after every read, she felt a little more pride than the last read; her motive was taking shape and this NGO was getting the best credit for its genuine work. Now she was bored, alone. She needed something to cheer herself up.

The moment she let herself into the northwest room of the villa on the second floor, Mannu started to thump his legs rapidly on the wooden floor and growling. His growl was loud enough to be heard in the farm, but there were none to hear his painful grunts. He recognized her entry even in half sleep; he was chained to a strange set of apparatus. The mechanism looked to be projected in a style that could support his whole torso, hook it upwards with a push of a button or if wished, tear it apart from all corners. A strange set of chains were locked to both his arms and feet. At first, his whole physical structure was at ease along the adjacent seat which was a component of this mechanism too, for him to breathe. However, the time had come for him to pay for all the sins he had committed on little Noori. To his utter surprise, he didn't understand why this Anaya was torturing him for the last ten months, but also took good care of him to withstand this painful process.

The process of begging, pledging and swearing for mercy was long gone. He knew that she was not going to stop until she satisfied herself. He just wished that it happened sooner rather than later and she would let him die. The usual buttons were pushed and the machine came to life, pulling apart the left side of his body away from his right side. The pain was immense and was tearing him from the middle. To his misery, Anaya had trashed his vocal cord long ago, so that his pain wouldn't be relieved by screaming and of course no one could hear his misery. The machines stopped after a while, just to flex

Mannu's muscles for the beating with a leather belt embedded with spikes. This was Anaya's daily routine, as if she enjoyed punishing him in the same way repeatedly. She wished to beat him, daily without rest, so that his old spots become red on his skin. Then there were twenty or thirty different ways of how she processed thereafter. Much depended on her mood, how happy she felt that very day. The happier she was, the more torturous the process became. And today she was quite happy. The day when Mannu would be tortured the most with his balls being crushed together for hours. His testicles were now just a means to urinate, and of course, it was a way of providing unbearable pain to his soul.

She came out of the room around nine, satisfied and fresh for the day ahead. At the dinner table, she sat down for a huge breakfast along with her accomplice Rituparna. Rituparna's face had an unremarkable spark, as if she had found her reason to live. Anaya still remembered the day she opened the gate for her, of this farmhouse for the first time. Anaya had revamped Rituparna from top to bottom; she was not some local young woman anymore. Rituparna had an unknown grudge towards the Border Security Force of the Indian army, camped in Itanagar. She never mentioned it to Anaya, but Anaya was smart enough to turn her anger in the way she needed. From then on, it was just small, small official formalities to arrange for Rituparna to officially register as a co-founder of the NGO after a month of Mannu's tragic accident. No wonder that the accident had just been a bogus step to make this entire process look legitimate for the modest people of Itanagar. Rituparna was more than happy to become her accomplice knowing that she could do all the aid work and help these poor tribes from being swindled by the Indian Army. She also helped justify Anaya's presence in the farmhouse anonymously.

"Ritu, send a telegram to my uncle in London requesting him to send some more funds, before distributing these new supplies at Manabhum Reserve Forest in the Changlang District. It's been over a month since we reached those people, I wonder if those Hrusso people have even begun using those medicines."

"Sure."

In reply to her telegram, a phone call landed at the villa around 9 p.m. after a week. It was Shariff, whose call originated from Pakistan to London, then later re-routed to Itanagar.

"Anaya, how are you?"

"Chachu, your return gift is ready!"

"Gift, what's that! Did you kill him?"

"No, he is alive and well. If I were just to obliterate him, I would have long back."

"Then tell me at least what are you up to. Why so much secrecy?"

"Okay… okay! I have formed a proper chain of my own people here. This NGO will be a perfect cover for your group to fund the people here. All I need are a few experts – Fedayeens who can brainwash these tribes to form a militant group who will fight for our cause. I need an explosion, arms, and medical experts, and yes, one should be female Fedayeen."

"Hmm, I will ring my ISI contacts and get a few Fedayeen ready."

"No rush, Chachu. Meanwhile, I have planned something big. Have you reviewed the courier I sent you?"

"Yes, it's quite detailed. I am going to share this one with my group tomorrow at the clubhouse."

When she spoke, she concluded the meeting with a note, "These people will fight the war for us, and trust me, I will wound this bloody country piece by piece."

"*Insha Allah! Meri bachi*, may god be with you!

"Don't think Allah has any role in it." Then she disconnected the call, even before Shariff could bid her goodbye.

◆

Islamabad, Pakistan
Following day
Around 7 p.m.

Every member of the Elaf Club was seated comfortably on their designated leather couches, with his own preferred drinks at adjacent tables. Most of them preferred tea, but Shariff accompanied it by rum and a handmade cigarette. Shariff was the honourable president of this group. He had formed this group just after his retirement, and all of the members had one common obsession, India. The members of this regime were retired officials, like ISI Chief Bashir Ahmed, retired general of Pakistan armed forces, Ex-Reserve Bank of Pakistan's chief (RBP), the other two were retired from active politics, but had their sharp teeth clawed into the ruling government and opposition, and at the end of the index was the oil king of Pakistan, Amir Mahboob Javeri. This group formed and portrayed itself as an old bunch of retired officials to play poker and enjoy their retirement, but they were a bunch of old radicals who wanted

to spice up their own sad ending. Some of them had their own
personal grudges like Shariff, but most of them were here to
keep their tab on the country and have access to its billions of
liquid money and resources. These old radicals were in a process
to construct something that very day of December 1992, which
would be far worse than just a conflict between two nations.

It all started with studying the thirteen locations for hours,
highlighting on the map of Mumbai then called Bombay, India's
economy centre. No one talked in between; it was Elaf group's
way of dealing with the proposal or any strategy. After all, every
individual was experienced enough to think from every angle and
arranging recourses to the consequence and then the outcome
of the conspiracy, by themselves. There were few diverse ideas
which came from different members, such as why not Delhi,
why Bombay? Also why only these locations, why not Gateway
of India as well?

For which Shariff already had a satisfying answer. And
finally, late in the night, they all agreed to bomb Bombay. Such
a massive attack had never been carried out before, and surely
would pose as a terrorist act to avenge Babri Masjid, which had
occurred a few days earlier. Their plan was heralding the darkest
era of the Indians. After all, when two brothers fight for a piece
of bread, there will always be a third, smarter dog to steal it
from them. Therefore, the Bombay blast expected to deliver
its utmost, the retired ISI chief suggested to bring in the IRA
(Irish Republican Army), then believed to be an expert in such
terrorist acts.

Shariff also made it clear that to succeed and continue
destroying this democratic nation, they needed to be very sure

of choosing the correct string of marionettes, who could then further recruit such similar people. The retired RBP chief along with the oil king started to raise funds with their Saudi contacts who had enough money to play an expensive game for the sake of fun. This was indeed just a game for them. It was a well-known fact, now that these Saudi royals never cared for any Muslims other than their own Muslim nations. When they heard of such a plan, they knew this would toss these two poor nations furthermore in poverty, which will result in only one thing – more human resources slaving in Saudi.

After months of preparation, the plan was formulated and a creepy idea now took the shape of a huge blueprint. The blueprint now had thirteen different sections with each target noted from top to bottom with every resource available on their place, along with a note of their designated assignment. One of the Saudi investors suggested a name that was later finalized as the main facilitator of the resources; Elaf group never knew this man before and didn't object for two reasons. First, it was a recommendation from a Saudi prince; and the second, also far more interesting fact was that the facilitator was an Indian, named Dawood Ibrahim. It could be anything, but at the Elaf group table, it was suspected that the facilitator wanted to stretch his own boundaries of just being a small-time smuggler to be a don in the international underworld. One thing was also clear to them – Dawood was just a businessman. He didn't care or give a damn about avenging any communal purpose. He just wanted to make his own fortune out of these communal conflicts in India, and the man was impressive from day one. In his own team, he had his own brainwashed, economically weaker background and emotionally persuaded marionettes to join operations allegedly as revenge for the Babri mosque demolition.

13th March 1993

Anaya ran towards the sealed room in the basement of the cottage of the Tegi Farmhouse with a newspaper in hand. Eventually, Anaya was also bored with the routine of torturing him twice every day. The day she got bored, she broke his spinal cord to paralyze him permanently and he had been bedridden ever since. Mannu knew that his end would not come easily from his abductor. From then on, he waited, simply waited to die.

As soon as she opened the door, she saw a man on a wooden cot, covered with a few blankets. The man's physical appearance was gaunt. The flesh between the bones and the skin was all gone with the kind of third-degree torture he was getting from Anaya. His head was bald, and it seemed like all his hair was falling out because of weakness. His eyes were staring at the ceiling, a blank look in them. She came near the half-dead creature eagerly and flashed a news article in front of his face. "Look Mannu Uncle… look!"

The newspaper had a bold headline on the front page, which read:

Bombay hit by a devastating series of 13 bombs

About 257 people were killed and over 700 injured in a series of explosions that rocked Bombay yesterday.

Her eyes had a sparkle, and the effect got heightened when she didn't get back the answer she wanted. She never knew what victory meant. What she had achieved today had to be and needed to be cherished. Usually, this villa only reverberated with the screams of a man, but today he didn't have that fear in his eyes. So, the villa heard the cries of a female for the first time. She realised her captive might have left his body a long time ago. Anaya hadn't visited Mannu for almost two weeks now. She was the only one who took care of this man personally. She kept him alive on a diet which was just sufficient for survival. She then noticed his bed having quite a few worms crawling on it. She further noticed the smell the stench of flesh in the room. She grabbed Mannu and turned him around to see. She was disturbed to see the bedsore riddled with earthworms and insects. She left him as it is, and walked backwards until she hit the nearby wall. Looking at his end suddenly gave her the feeling of being freed from captivity in which she had unknowingly trapped herself.

Next day, Moolchand Tegi's sudden death was published in the daily mail.

Some days later, she found herself amused by the fact that the Indian RAW and local police could have foiled her whole plan. A man named Gullu was in the process of leaking out information about the location of the thirteen bombs, but the concerned authorities simply ignored it.

From then on, Anaya rode wild on the back of her old radical puppets, the Elaf group, executing many attacks in India. Her masterful deceptive plans led to the failure of the Indian Intelligence RAW every time. In between, the period of ten years, many more extremists such as Lashkar-e-Taiba and Jaish-e-Mohammed joined hands without knowing the actual perpetrator. She kept her cover intact, roaming around India, looking for the next target. The attack on the Indian Parliament and Akshradham remained her crown jewels by the end of 2002. The fact that she had decided to create such an extremist external group for a purpose, the purpose of these suicidal missions, was to leave its wounded mark on every Indian heart. She wanted every Indian to feel insecure, unsafe and worried for the rest of their lives. Her mind was full of pride for pushing herself to the limits of insanity.

On the other side, Shariff was worried; worried about her niece who was getting a little more tentative and aggressive with her methods and executions. She was hitting Indians quite frequently and was not giving enough time to prepare her plan, which necessitated for her to be out there in the open without her guards quite often. He had a bad feeling, because there were quite a number of attacks, which looked false-killing only one or two, here and there. This was enough to provoke her for the next attack. And one strange fact was that the numbers of fatalities were large in the last few attacks. As if someone was intentionally feeding a false figure. Anaya was feeling extremely happy with those figures, but Shariff somehow traced a resemblance to their time in 1971. He tried to make her understand his thoughts, but in return he only got a standard answer, "Chachu, you are getting old," and for the first time, she laughed in his face. He felt ransacked, stripped naked by his own creation.

"You will never know when they hit you – that's their specialty," he tried to tell her.

Part – II

One

The Red, Spy

Budapest, CIA Headquarters
24th September

The day started, as ordinary as it should be. Tracking all the clear and present dangers arising from the European region, handling asset transfers, tracking every active agent in this part of the world of MFS (German secret service), KGB, now proudly known as FSB, French security services, the Ukrainians, and other well-known American pals in the world of espionage. They track and keep their eye on every bit of movement in this area. It's their normal routine, schedule or protocol – call it whatever, – along with a sip of the morning coffee at the basement floors of an American nationalized bank.

Madelyn's elite, controlling every bit of a five-kilometre radius of the CIA HQs, now occupied the topmost floors of the adjacent building. Most of the American bank staff was unaware of the fact that they had all been scrutinized intimately since the previous night. Every bit of their life was watched and checked thoroughly to see if they had been manipulated or had been used as a key to get into the HQ. This unknown man had now become the top priority for the team to track down. Madelyn got an early morning confirmation call from her team that the Indian diplomat Gopal had dropped a small microchip with all the necessary information about the building being used as the CIA HQ. Madelyn ordered to leave the chip exactly where they had found it and vanish. She didn't want anyone to know that she had gained an upper hand. The 'Eagles' were the eyes and the ears of this deadly trap. Equipped to the core, scanning every individual by not only his or her face, but with his or her posture, gait everything.

The hit and grab team called 'Alpha' armed with guns and injections filled with anaesthetic liquid were boots on the ground. They neutralized the subjects, flagged by the Eagle. Team Alpha consisted of thirty men and women and was scattered around the area like ants.

Then there was a three-member team inside the CIA HQ, command operation post for Eagle and Alpha. If by any means the man from RAW managed to come into the lion's den, then the lioness would be happy to greet him personally. Madelyn never left her office since the day before; she preferred to freshen up inside the office and changed to something comfortable, yet professional looking. Matt still wore the same outfit and so did John, her two senior-most officers.

The day passed by with a couple of false flags. Everything looked extraordinarily calm, leaving a hurricane inside Madelyn. Was she missing something? What was it?

The evidence showed otherwise. Someone had tried to manipulate her and the team of experts of CIA, first when all of her resources ran around the city following Gopal and then today. Was she losing her touch?

Her shoulders were down by midnight, but her mind was racing with all kinds of thoughts. She had only managed to get a glimpse of the man once, and that was when she saw that hooded man in the opera house. She again started watching the video feeds. She was observing every angle acutely. Until the feeds stopped in the middle and the second feed loaded, but she saw that the timer on the last feed and the present feed with a difference.

"What was that? What just happened? Why are we missing out on thirty seconds?"

The nerds looked at each other.

"We had an issue with the router, so I had to reboot it," the senior one responded.

"Would you mind explaining why your router had such an issue while we were in such a high profile pursuit of a suspect?"

"I am not sure, but it acted strangely and cut us off, stating one foreign device was detected inside the Web. I mean how can that happen, right?"

She hauled him by his collar and took them to the Web, parked one floor below. Matt followed them without invitation. Inside the Web, they found a phone connected to a small device. It looked as if someone had slipped it in a hurry. The senior was quick to spot his chance of proving his usefulness connecting it to the laptop and running a script.

He subsequently told his female boss that this device was used as bridge to copy files remotely, 1.5 GB in total. A substantial about of data.

Strangely, in this situation, Madelyn had a scary laugh and said, "Impeccable!"

She gave a glare to Matt. She left the scene, knowing that she was hacked into the day before itself, and that the man did not intend to pay a visit today. He set up this trap for them to focus on preventing the hack, when right now, he must have easily slipped out of the country. It was a master deception to create a full illusion.

When Matt came to Madelyn's chamber later, he found her ready to leave. He had never seen her like this since he had known her in the field. Her face had a defeated look, her shoulders drooped, and he could see that she was in shock.

Before leaving, she requested Matt, "Please call off the manhunt after an hour." She avoided all eye contact.

"You can't blame yourself, Madelyn. You are not the only one who has been beaten by this bastard," Matt paused in between, and concluded by saying, "We all are."

She left saying, "I know. I just need a little rest."

It was 4 a.m. when she reached her hotel, at 1051 street, Erzsébet Square – Le Méridien. She ordered the female receptionist for a bottle of scotch.

The receptionist sent a bellhop with a bottle of William Grant, her preferred scotch. To her knowledge, Madelyn was Sophia Walker, a marketing head of the American Nationalized bank. The receptionist went back to the small room behind the reception area and called someone.

Somewhere not far away from Le Méridian, the phone call landed shrilly, disturbing the sleep of a man, aged around forty with a scruffy grey beard and grey hair. He barely spoke on the phone except for saying *"Grazie"* when he thanked for the information he got from the receptionist. They both spoke Italian.

He put down the receiver and stretched his body to the full, yawning. He noticed that his latest love was also up, thanks to the sudden phone call. He got up and sat straight on the bed with his own pillow to rest his back. The Italian saw his partner lighting up a cigarette. His lower body was half covered with the bedsheet and one thigh was out of it. His boyfriend was a lot younger than he was. The Italian smiled at him and spoke in a soft voice, "The woman returned to her suite." He turned his back to his partner, "Sleep now if you have to catch her tomorrow first."

"Sure… you go ahead, take a nap sweetheart… and thanks for all of this."

The Italian responded in a sleepy voice, "You thanked me enough last night, charming."

Arya looked in the mirror and felt exploited that he had shared a bed with a man. This job was turning him upside down; he knew he shouldn't feel in such a way. It's just what was needed, and it was the only way to keep a tab on Madelyn. He was fighting alone, so he had to take some extraordinary routes to achieve his goal.

The day before when he was ditched by Aisha, he put together the broken pieces and understood going into battle against elite team at Frankfurt was far more dangerous than going after

Madelyn. He knew that she had the highest clearance in this case and only she could provide him what he needed – Farooq!

His biggest advantage was that he had managed to hide his identity from everyone. They didn't know him by his face and so he had a chance in this battle. He knew Madelyn's car number, so as soon as he landed back in Budapest from Vienna, he searched every five-star hotel near Bank Street, where the CIA HQ was located, tipped parking lot attendants to see if anyone of them knew this plate driven by an Afro-American woman. The bribery always worked, and there was no harm just to say yes or no for $10. Then later in the evening, he searched and monitored all the hotel staff to look for a man or woman who had control over the rest of the staff; it was front desk manager. He found his man, an Italian named Niccolaio Moretti.

Blackmail, kidnapping and other forceful acts of violence were his options, but he knew these weren't safe methods. He didn't have time for it, once CIA realized that they were being played at, first with Gopal and then the false HQ breach hooks, Madelyn might feel the need to leave Budapest. In both the cases, Arya would lose at the onset. He assumed he had twenty to forty-eight hours. With all these thoughts, he trailed Niccolaio to his apartment; he soon came to know that this Italian lived alone, so the threatening and blackmailing with his near and dear ones were out of the question. He then saw this man wear a flashy blue shirt and a white paint suit before going out again, to spend the rest of his evening. The Italian entered a bar called Peaches with the glossy board, which made it perfectly clear that this Italian was in fact interested in men rather than women.

There was no other choice, Arya had thought long and hard to find any other way. He approached him inside the bar, and then he manipulated Niccolaio's feelings and hooked him into a honey trap. Niccolaio was soon convinced that this stranger was a freelance detective and had come to Budapest for an important assignment. The nature of his job attracted Niccolaio more as it was quite dangerous at times, as told by Arya. By the time they finished their drinks and dinner at the Peaches, Niccolaio couldn't resist him and asked him to stay at his place. Arya gracefully accepted this and after a lavishing rendezvous in bed with Niccolaio, Arya continued some phony story about his latest assignment and how he had lost track of a woman he was pursuing. Niccolaio couldn't resist but to ask the identity of this woman. He showed Madelyn's picture and told him her name, but the Italian corrected him saying that her name was Sophia Walker and she was a guest at his hotel. Arya then convinced him saying that she was hiding with an alias identity and he must help him to expose her. Niccolaio at first was a little hesitant, but after a few more strokes of love and passion, he agreed.

It's been almost a day since she had returned to her suite at Le Méridian, and hadn't left it since. The Italian manager arranged for his lover Arya to be in a suite opposite to Madelyn's, in exchange for further encounters in bed. Arya kept a tab on her, along with the front desk receptionist. The day passed without any movement from Madelyn, and she only opened her doors to receive her lunch, dinner and an occasional coffee. Every time she opened her door, Arya got a glimpse of a woman in her white robe, through the keyhole. It was at two at night when

Arya decided to put his guard down and found comforting sleep an hour after watching TV.

The next morning at 8:45, there was a loud knock on the door to disturb his peaceful sleep. He woke up with a start and saw through the peephole a woman employee standing and knocking at the door. She spoke with a smile, "Miss Walker is scheduled to check out at nine today; your taxi is waiting outside," and left. He needed to hurry up, and get ahead of Madelyn. In his own hurry, he noticed he had forgotten to switch off the TV. He picked up the remote to switch it off – the BBC panel were debating on the horrifying image of the scattered houses, along with six dead people. He easily recognized one of the faces as Farooq. He stopped to see that the reporter publicly accused the Indian intelligence agency RAW of being involved in this devious act, of so-called cleaning their mess after Budapest. Arya switched off the crap and left the room. He saw Madelyn waiting for the lift at the end of the hallway. He progressed towards the emergency exit, jumping across the stairs like a baboon. It took him merely a minute to reach the ground floor and he managed to be ahead of Madelyn. He waited in his taxi arranged by his lover Niccolaio, for her to come out of the hotel.

Few minutes later, Madelyn came out with her Audi and drove straight, opposite to the direction of the CIA HQ.

Only Aisha knew about Frankfurt, he thought during his pursuit. He had told her the location of Farooq himself. Either CIA blew up their own safe house or Aisha had tipped her handlers. The second option was more plausible. Then why was Arya following Madelyn? To know for sure. In his line of work, anything can be manipulated to look legitimate. Arya was always the one who believed in his hunch and intelligence rather than some fuzzy report.

Arya changed his taxi, to keep up the tail undetected. On the other hand, Madelyn was certain that nobody had followed her till she made her final stop at a neighbourhood in the Buda side of Budapest. It was an area full of apartments, not so far from the Danube river. She went inside one of them and came out after ten minutes. She looked around scanning the neighbourhood. Once she had the confidence that she was not being looked at, she dialled a number and spoke something. In a distance, Arya could only gather by the movement of her lips "Will evac in two hours." He cursed himself for not carrying binoculars.

This society with common looking apartments was typical and looked uninhabited. Even the wind was silent on this cloudy, chilly day.

In one of the apartments numbered 363, a ponytailed man dressed in cargo pants, T-shirt, and an overcoat came out of the room, closing the door and leaving behind a man strapped to a steel chair stark naked. The ponytailed man was sweating like a pig and had a stone face. The man who was left behind was chubby and had body hair covering most of his brown skin. He was Farooq, tired of beating around the clock. His nails were snatched out from all his fingers. His ears, nose, and left collarbone looked severely injured.

The ponytailed man nodded negatively to his superior that he couldn't get any more information other than what they already knew. He went back to interrogate Farooq. The captain of the team went back to his novel with a Cuban cigar stuck between his lips. By looking at his face, anyone would know that he was a veteran of some sort. He had been doing enough dirty work of breaking the human soul with harsh brutality and earned great respect among the new recruits in this dirty little world of espionage. He didn't get his hands dirty till it was most needed. There was a time back in the olden days when an agent on the field was always the one to wash his own hands with the captives' blood.

In the modern world of espionage, an elite team usually got such assignments. They fly in and fly out with the experts in interrogation technique and psychology. Since they specialized in the department of breaking the human soul, their methods were usually not limited to beating. They had other psychological methods of torturing. This team is such a special task force that has unlimited powers. No questions asked, no answers expected. The members including the captain looked soulless. There were three other personnel in the room; one was listening to the sophisticated looking radios placed in the hall, with headphones. The fourth and the fifth were simply extra force, muscular and at their supreme attention, securing the windows. Needless to say, the room had enough firepower to fight a small army. The whole apartment had rigged doors, windows, even ceilings. One forced entry and the whole kill squad would go boom along with the intruder.

The captain looked at his watch; there was still an hour left for them to leave the place.

Suddenly, the man on the radio dropped his headphone and informed his captain that the police was going to raid the building to catch a suspected arms dealer. He was listening to all the police channels to see how safe their area was. The captain ran towards the room and ordered the ponytailed man to wrap up. He then liquidated Farooq, who was in enough pain already and wanted something to reduce it for a long time. They were out, quick and quiet. From the moment they left the apartment until they safely sat inside the car, all of them formed a tight perimetre around their captive. They walked briskly, pointing their weapons at every single inch of space on their way. The radioman gave confirmation to the captain that there were no long-range snipers on the roofs within a twenty-mile radius, according to the latest satellite feeds. They would not have left the apartment until three, but the apartment that they were using was about to make headlines on every news channel because of the local police raid. The engine came to life as the captain signalled to the ponytailed man in the driver seat to proceed to their destination sitting right next to him. Farooq was in the middle row and seated in between the two arms specialists. The radioman occupied the last seat in the armored vehicle. As their vehicle came out of the basement and crossed the empty yard of the building, a young boy on his bicycle noticed their high speed. The boy saw them clearly, till they took a left turn quarter mile straight ahead and joined the traffic. He drew out a brand new phone and looked excited while dialling a number, "Hello Mister, they went down the exact way as you said. Now is this phone mine?"

The kid had unknowingly acted as an informant.

The captain in the armed convoy looked confident as they took a turn on Sezermi way and headed for the 'Rakoczi hid' – one of the many bridges which interconnect Buda to the Pest part of this city. The man in the back seat of the car just reported their exact location on the route to their man waiting near the metro station on the other side of the bridge and stated that they were two minutes away from the rendezvous point. He then ordered him to get the boat ready. They drove past a man on a motorbike driving ahead of them with his partner in the back seat. The female companion on the bike looked surprised as the car passed by them in a hurry. The captain looked at them from the rear view and noticed that the bike driver hurriedly stopped the bike as if he had seen something. They were so focused on their path ahead that the driver of the car had missed seeing a construction truck that had entered from a sub connector pass, joining the main sezermi way just behind them. The construction truck was running as if it had lost control of its own speed, so the biker had stopped at once to save his life. The captain was the first to spot this unexpected monster heading towards the car, totally out of control. However, there was no time left for them to step aside or avoid the collision. The truck hit the back of the car, forcing it off the road. The passenger in the back of the car lost his senses with the collision, though the car was steady on the road, because of its features. However, before the driver could gain any control, the truck behind them hit even harder. Then everyone in the car grabbed whatever they could to prevent themselves from being thrown out. It finally lost its control lifting its wheels, and did a somersault once before standing back on its feet horizontally, standing in between the bridge. If the truck did hit them now, it would be on the captain's side. The ponytailed driver came back to his senses and tried to start the car. The captain looked at his driver's helpless act, and looked back at the monster truck heading their way. The driver of the construction truck was doing it purposely.

The truck hit them with a force so powerful that it made a crack in the armed bulletproof window glass on the side of the captain. The car did its best to stay put, but there wasn't enough metal to hold it against the truck, so it slid off. The shrouded driver did it very efficiently, dragging it towards the edge of the bridge. The captain made eye contact with the truck's driver, but there was nothing he could do now. The truck driver smashed them against the cemented corner of the bridge and throwing them off the grid. The car was on its way to the deep waters below the bridge. The captain hadn't stopped looking at the truck, calmly at his unknown enemy, who was now driving the truck towards the broken edge of the bridge.

The whole accident was clearly witnessed by the biker and his female companion. To them, the truck had lost control and hit the car with a few passengers in it, and the accident threw the car into the water. There was a huge spray of water when the car hit the water. It floated for a few seconds before sinking. They also saw the truck hanging on the bridge like a seesaw, with its driver holding and hanging himself from the open doorknob. He grabbed something and then left the handle of the door, diving straight into the water. The biker ran towards the edge of the broken bridge and searched for any survivors, but there were none.

It took three seconds to clear the bubbles when the shrouded driver reached under the water. As soon as the bubbles cleared, Arya removed his shroud and spotted the car sinking deep and deep into the core of the Danube river. He took a deep dive towards the car, swimming rapidly to gain speed.

With the help of a power metre, Arya had narrowed down the apartment which was consuming the highest electrical usage. Equipment used by such an elite team consumed ten times more power than a normal household does. He searched and saw this convoy in the basement. The more he looked at the convoy, the more he was convinced that the team guarding Farooq would not leave any loose ends to release Farooq from their grip. There was no point taking them head on. Arya was outnumbered and outgunned from the start. The only chance to extract Farooq out would be when they were in a tight equation, which would be in this car. He knew the team would extract Farooq in time because the CIA was sure that their fake safe house at Frankfurt was hit earlier that day and their bid was successful. Now the real Farooq needed to be out of Budapest, into their own territory. Aisha had helped Arya unknowingly, for which he promised himself that he would pay his debt on their next encounter.

Arya needed something to divert the elite from their normal course. That's why he wrongly tipped the local authorities about some high profile arms dealer being in the same building as Farooq. The trick worked and he was able to coerce the whole team into the water. But his worries started now. The armoured car was made so secure that no bullet could hit the mark. The windows couldn't be broken from inside as well to get out, especially when the doors were jammed because of the hit. Further to his disadvantage, the way the car was releasing bubbles meant that there might be a permanent hole somewhere in the car, which must be filling with water rapidly and would surely run out of oxygen any moment. Arya needed to find a way soon. He swam faster to reach the car and saw the ponytailed driver swimming furiously out of the vehicle. He was the only one to come out, and passed by Arya, but did not notice him. He was in a rush to survive. When Arya reached the car, it was already at rest at the bottom of the river, wheels up. The door was unlocked, so he peeked under and saw Farooq. Was he dead? Arya didn't have time to think, he dragged him out of the convoy and fixed a small oxygen cylinder to pump in oxygen through his mouth. In a second or two, he saw him moving, but he couldn't swim on his own for sure. He also noticed that the captain was struggling with his last breaths in the front seat, leaving the last oxygen out in the form of bubbles. The other three were dead already. Farooq survived only because he was sitting in between, or because of him being heavily sedated, which had slowed down his senses to react to drowning. Arya tossed an oxygen cylinder to the captain for him to survive until the ponytailed guy came back. He'd come back for his captain, Arya thought. Arya shared a gaze with the captain, probably to convey, "It had to be done, and there was no other way".

He hadn't even gone a few metres when he heard a faint sound of a splash. The truck had also fallen from the bridge, landing on the car, crushing it under the muddy layer of the river.

Two

The Red, Defectors

March 2004
Gangtok, Sikkim

She had developed a wild pleasure of scouting every target before blowing it to pieces. She got extra satisfaction while doing so, scanning every human being in the place thinking whether that unknown man would be her next target or not. This time she had decided to do something different. Her area of attack was this small beautiful, untouched town. She chose this town because she wanted to cast a wide web in this country. It was the start of the summer of 2004, and that meant rain was quite common in this town surrounded by four hills. Anaya liked one thing, and that was walking alone in the rain. The water drops made her feel alive, and her feeling was only restricted to these raindrops; there was nothing else in the world, which made her feel anything remotely like what she felt at that moment.

It was around eight in the evening and she felt a little out of breath walking towards Lal market. She could see that it was only a few feet away, but her rapidly beating heart made her stop. She felt an urge to smoke, so she took shelter under a building next to the street. She brought out a pack of Marlboro from inside her brown leather overcoat and placed one on her lips. She then searched for a lighter in her other pocket. She almost missed seeing a hand, which advanced towards the tip of her cigarette with a flame. She turned with her full attention, and saw an elderly man. Due to the sudden electrical breakdown a few minutes ago, the whole area was dark. The man, she saw, was an older looking gentleman, with a grey moustache and well combed hair with black and grey shades. His cheeks sagged, and he had the eyes of an office clerk, tired but painless, as if he was used to this exhausting career. The lights were back on, and she thanked him for the flame. The man then lit his own with a stick taken from a matchbox embedded with 'The Oriental' on it. Must be his present bed and breakfast inn. Her guess about that man was kicked aside when that man replied, "It's okay Anaya!"

She didn't respond to that proactive hoary smoker. Her posture was calm and cool. Then the man spoke again, "Anaya, what's your plan for this city? How many targets to be bombed?"

Anaya stopped; she had to. This man had provoked her enough; she really dropped that nonsense and came to him. His elbow grabbed, the man felt a round hole was being pushed against his ribcage. The man looked down and confirmed it was a Glock 26 with a 19 mm parabellum. Rarest model to find, at least in the Indian subcontinent. When she spoke, he could sense her anger, "One push Mister, and this 19 mm will only take half a second to puncture your heart. You better—"

"Anaya, I really expected more out of you than this. What do you think of me, a burglar or what?" The man cut her short when he felt his own reputation was being ridiculed.

She didn't think it through, there was no time. Someone knew her being here was enough to cloud her judgment of the situation entirely. She dropped her stance, realizing the man had a valid point and needed to be heard.

They then found a joint, not so charming with shades of light which made everyone look as reddish as possible.

The old man took the seat first, and then she entered the cabin, which had an oversized table making it difficult to get in first. A boy came and took the order for plates of dumplings and beer, one for each. The order was placed without her consent, but the man couldn't care less.

"I need help to get out of this country. And I mean now. In return, I will help you live." The man had poor negotiation skills.

Anaya, "Okay who is going to kill me? And what makes you so sure that I want to live?"

"Oh come on, don't tell me bombing India was your final move."

"Did Shariff spell it out? Who are you?"

"I don't have the bloody time to fill up your questionnaire!" the man had raised his voice for the first time. He continued, "There is an elite team already on its way to assassinate everyone in the Elaf group. I am here because the approvals go through me."

The man whispered, "The fact that there is a girl, who is the brain behind Elaf and even this Jaish and Lashkar is not known to anyone yet, but me. It took me time to figure it out, but when I did it, tracking you here was easy."

Anaya kept being blown off by this chubby character with a clerical face and the man understood her confused face.

"Your work is impressive, controlling these radicals for your reasons. But don't tell me you underestimated RAW?"

She kept her silence. "Look, I can make you invisible once again, but you have to help me first, to get out of this country. My contacts are all jammed and avoiding me for quite some time, and I sense RAW is coming for me too! I need a way out from India."

Her own, newly grown superiority complex was not letting her believe the man. Her body language, however, was that of an amateur and the man had no tolerance for that.

He brought out a device with touch features, and a remotely connected device.

He toggled through and showed that the man only knew his business and was extremely good at it. It had all the evidence proving that a British national named Anaya McQuillen had been behind every bombing since '93.

The man spoke again, "This little secret of yours will be buried if you help me out."

Her vivid mind was still puzzled by that evidence. If this man was intelligent enough to find her all alone, couldn't he rescue himself? Who was he anyway? And why was he running?

She voiced her questions.

"You're not asking the right questions, darling. The real question would be why I choose to let a bloody terrorist slip away?"

She felt offended but knew her time would come, soon. The man then started to brag about the way he had found her. That was the problem. The moment you feel proud of yourself in this business, that very moment your clock starts ticking towards your end. Like it did for Anaya.

Thimphu, Bhutan
Following day

By noon, Anaya and the shady nameless character crossed the Indian border to Bhutan and found themselves in a city bus en-route to Thimphu. But they made sure to leave a false trail behind, of leaving Sikkim for Nepal.

The man was less paranoid now and felt a little assured of his survival. After all, the dutiful Anaya had ensured their safe passage out of India. The bus was full of locals and it was safe to chat in Hindi.

"When will you destroy that evidence?"

"As soon as I feel safe and secure."

Anaya rolled her fingers on the man's cheek, and said, "You are safe now."

"Anaya, save your bitchy traps for those who are interested, not me." She felt a tight slap on her cheek in turn.

"If I am the bitch, then who are you supposed to be? A traitor or a coward?"

"I did serve my country till I felt so, and now I don't. Is it so hard for everyone to understand? If my country is my mother, then I am sure she will understand her son. The CIA allowed me to defect because I am the best in the lot and I did pull you down to your knees, didn't I?"

These were the last words between the two, until they reached the capital. In between, when the bus stopped for refreshments, Anaya had a talk with Shariff. She brought him up to date in two minutes and got a confirmation that indeed a group member Amir Mahboob Javeri, oil king of Pakistan had been found dead in his farmhouse. The early reports were that his heart pumped a little too fast than it should when the horny king got escort services to satisfy his ageing needs. There was heroin found in his blood and the reporter first at the scene concluded that the king wanted to take his female escort places with that heavy dose. The defector was correct, the assassination team was lethal and faster then she presumed.

Shariff told her that one of his contacts, Jan Mohammad Baloch a.k.a 'Mir' would extract them from Bhutan. They got off the phone telling each other to take care, which meant not to be killed.

They navigated to the only airport in the country once they reached the city of hamlets. The defector confirmed with an older looking officer that the airport had received an urgent request for a charter to land for refuelling. The old officer seemed chuffed about the request since only eight pilots in the world were certified to land at the Paro Airport, because of its extreme geographical location. This airport is basically just an asphalt stripe surrounded by the Himalayas, with extreme meteorological conditions, and at an altitude of 2,236 metres, putting it at number one in the list of hot landing zones. In other words, the officer was sure that they won't be able to land in such a situation and he looked unsure and surprised by how this charter got approval.

It was around four in the evening when Anaya called Shariff to confirm whether he got a deal with his contact Mir, but Shariff didn't pick up the call even after many tries. She didn't want to think of the consequences. Shariff was the only shelter under which she survived and ruled for such a long time, and if he was taken out, then she was just a kite without thread. Shariff had also told her during the last call that Syria would be safe for a while, for her and the defector.

Anaya looked at the dusk-dawn skyline while sitting on a wooden box waiting for its shipment. She raised the collar of her jacket to cover her ears, which felt numb in the cold breeze. The defector walked round and round continuously, but had a shiver and a funny stride. They surely were a little underdressed for Bhutan and were waiting for the charter to land. They saw the outline of a charter plane flying in the area, but couldn't spot it in the hazy sky. According to the officer, he had given a green signal twenty minutes ago, and the pilot must be trying his best to land the plane in one piece.

He was the first to spot the charter at the edge of the skyline and was shocked to see the attempt. The charter came rushing and oscillating, rolling from one of the mountain edges and finally, its back wheels touched the tarmac, and then flew up. The pilot tried to stay on the ground twice after that, but every time the concentrated air was pushing the charter up in the air and finally, the tarmac came to its end on the side of the spectators – Anaya, the defector and the lone airport officer. The pilot flew up just before he would crash into the pile of wooden boxes on which Anaya was sitting. It flew around the valley, swinging back and forth, to and fro, and tried its luck to land again. This time he was able to pull off the unbelievable task as the officer exclaimed loudly, making him the ninth pilot person to land safely, uncertified though it was. After thirty minutes roughly, the pilot did the unbelievable task to be airborne, leaving the airport officer on the tarmac sitting on the steel chair alone. His constant eyes watched them vanish into the heavens as a small cat licked the dripping blood on the ground near his seat.

The defector threw up thrice, excusing himself because of the turbulent take-off. The pilot came out of his cabin when they crossed the Himalayas. Gliding above Afghanistan or neighbouring Tajikistan, the dryer range of brownish landscape was devoid of greenery. The pilot looked happy at his own achievement and inquired what he could do to make his customer's further journey as painless as possible. As requested, the pilot brought out some packed meals with a bottle of vodka and the famished defector took the heavy dose and sunk into a deep sleep. Abu Dhabi was their destination, before finally reaching Syria. When he woke up, Anaya was not in her seat, but instead came out of the cockpit. The defector looked at her cunningly and said, "Enjoyed?"

She replied, "I was getting bored listening to your snoring, so I thought it's better to appreciate the man who flew us out. He was exhausted…." Then she giggled.

A group of Americans took the defector away as soon as they landed in Abu Dhabi. However, before he left, he kept his promise to Anaya and her existence was scrapped off from the RAW database remotely. Her peaceful extradition lasted until she reached Damascus, Syria. Mir kept her captive since Shariff had never paid his dues. Shariff was never again spotted by anyone; he had gone missing. With no help or sign of help in the near future, she did all she could to survive by serving a man who turned out to be another kind of a molester.

She became someone's play tool again. A solicit.

◆

Farooq came back to his senses and took some time to focus on his surroundings; the more he focused, the more he got a headache. A hand rested on his shoulders and a blurred face came into his visibility. He looked exactly like the man who gave him oxygen under water. Farooq felt dryness all around and the discomfort was still unbearable. He tried to call out for water, but couldn't. The man understood Farooq's need and gave him a few drops of water. As soon as the water slid into his throat, Farooq felt better, but dizzier, and without his own realization, fainted again. He was led to the armed chair with the saline drip attached to his arms. His condition was stable, but far from normal. The more Arya looked at his bruises, the more he was convinced that this veteran had a strong temperament to hold whatever he was holding. However, to Arya, he was the key essential to solve or rather start solving this puzzle. *Who is this unseen fiend who was after RAW?*

It was an abandoned cottage in a small forest, thirty miles away from Budapest. He sat in his chair. It was a full moon night, and the forest was in silence, but Arya was restless. With each passing minute, he was getting a little paranoid; he knew how his whole team was dragged into this international conflict with the CIA. He wanted to know why the killer team of Ukrainians hunted him down. The whole point of this was just to frame RAW? By whom? A faceless clandestine organization? ISI? Aisha? Nah that girl didn't have it in her. She could be a pawn, but this was something else. Though, it was also clear that she was involved in this plan somehow. It couldn't be all coincidences.

Arya murmured to himself, "He has to talk."

He heard a distant howl of a wolf. Thinking of wolves, the characteristics matched with the person inside. Farooq had betrayed them all, a wolf insider. He looked at his watch; it had been twenty hours since they had arrived here and Farooq was still in the same condition. Was he faking it to gain time, the time he needed to…? Arya stood up, moved towards the room promptly. He opened the door quickly, but before he could spot his captive, a wooden strip flew towards his forehead. Arya was in no position to handle this attack, so he only managed to place his elbow to save the beating on his forehead.

Bang!

The wood cracked, and cracked hard on his elbow. The attack was strong enough to get him off balance. His head was still reeling with that crackerjack of the wood. When he saw Farooq limping, Arya touched his temple with his fist and saw the blood.

Arya drew his gun out. Two shots towards Farooq's shoulder as if he was doing target practice. Farooq instantly found himself on the ground; the wood in his hand fell on his forehead. Full of pain – but no bullet holes or blood. He coughed and grunted hard.

"Ow…ow… A beanbag round? Seriously?" He rolled over to his belly to find some relief. "Are they not giving any training on manners these days in the DIA?" He laughed as if he enjoyed this humour.

Arya didn't find it amusing, nor felt it necessary to respond to his sarcasm. He dragged Farooq inside again and forced him to sit on the same chair.

"Nice place. It's to my satisfaction. A bed and a breakfast would have given you my vote for the best interrogator."

"Glad you like it!" He strapped him with a cable to the chair and pulled it hard, clinching Farooq's foot.

"Easy… easy soldier…"

"You and I need to have a little chat…" Arya came closer, yet maintaining his distance.

"Is this an interrogation?" Farooq had a dirty smile on his face.

"That would be unprofessional, don't know think," replied Arya and Farooq saw his eyes deep and silent.

"I mean, if I can break you out of CIA… show me that you are still useful to me alive, than just dead."

To Arya's surprise, Farooq responded. "Establish your identity as an enforcer. That is… That is what number three… is not it. On the manual guide book on DIA?"

Arya knew this guy was a genius, and breaking a genius requires a lot of time – the basic ingredient of a successful interrogation, which he didn't have.

However, before he could start, Farooq said, "Don't even think about starting, how we're both on the same side and all that. I think my actions made it clear that I choose my own side.

"Sympathetic-Approach… number twenty, right?"

Arya said, "Yeah. And I got your point."

Arya changed his magazine round. This time it was a real one. Aiming at Farooq's head, and before Farooq could imagine what he was going to do, Arya fired a shot, missing him by an inch. However, for Farooq, it was like as if a bullet just went past his ears and dug into the back wooden wall. He was dazed.

Arya said, "How about this? You tell me, or I will shoot you point blank. You will not find that in any manual."

Farooq said, "You make it sound so personal, you don't know the reason for my betrayal."

Arya replied, "Then fill me in… I will try not to shoot until it gets boring."

Farooq began, "I was stationed with my family in Riyadh. An op went bad, and I lost my wife and son in a bid to escape. Before I could think of anything, I was in Turkey as a burnt asset, handling that horrible bar. Bureaucracy at its best! No formalities, nothing. To the organization, it was because of my casual approach that op failed. What did I get? My dead family on one hand and daily wages as a reimbursement. Then suddenly I got a call after twenty years. RAW needed my expertise once again. It was a way to get payback. I found what I was looking for."

Then there was a fleeting interruption as if he chose his words carefully before speaking out.

"It was RAW, my own people who were responsible for my suffering for the last twenty years."

Arya questioned, "You mean RAW killed your family?"

Farooq responded, "Oh come on, you know how it is. You are useful until you do as ordered, and maybe I crossed my line. So I was removed out of the loop, isolated, thrown away like an infected dog."

Arya smiled.

"How convenient? You will reach places, soldier," Farooq said annoyingly.

Arya said, "To my knowledge, you were never married. That wife and son you were blabbering about, they were just your cover family. Isn't it cute, Mr Balwinder Singh Chautala?"

Farooq shouted, "Bloody Brigadier! He couldn't keep a secret, could he?"

Farooq started again, "The op went bad because I had a wrong hunch, but that does not mean I was useless for the last twenty years. A soldier never dies of a bullet. He dies when his armour is seized away by the same people who once made him a soldier. Mir approached me before RAW. I chose my side with a lot of cash in my hand. I was again useful, at least for someone. I felt alive again. I was working as a double. It's exciting, isn't it?"

Arya had read it a thousand times in the white papers, SOPs, manuals on how human behaviour changes in this field.

However, this was the first time he got to see it through the eyes of a double agent. How easily he spelled it out, without a pinch of hesitation. There was no fear.

Farooq continued, "How he knew that RAW was coming to hunt him down? I can't say for sure. But he didn't care. I was on his side. I protected him from Virat, then one day, all of a sudden, I was contacted by a girl, and then I was offered to be a triple agent. Wow, the dirt I was waiting for to get my hands on. Misleading that bastard Virat, misleading Mir as an employee of the third party. Gosh! Supremacy of all."

Arya showed him a picture and asked," Is she the one?"

Farooq answered, "Yes… Aisha. Tempting, isn't she? I never understood how she was able to manipulate Mir and his whole network, being right under his nose."

Arya asked, "Are the folks that you work for a government agency or a foreign power? What are we up against?"

Farooq said, "Well, she never formally enrolled me on their payroll. No confidentiality act was signed? All I know is that they wanted to bring down RAW. My appetite whetted and I was being paid from three different corners. One couldn't complain."

Farooq sighed. "They could be multinational, hired gun or ISI. Why do I care?"

"An anti-RAW," Farooq saw Arya calculating every word coming out of his mouth.

"Shall I continue?" Farooq asked politely.

"The new role demanded me to play along with Mir and Virat at the same time. But then, something spooked Virat. He called you over, and before I could think, you somehow managed to get that chip before me and we landed up at Marcos' location. I was inches away from being blown off if you people had caught Marcos. At least to the extent that I was double and was sold out to Mir. Virat kept me with him on that night. I couldn't sneak out; it was dangerous. Fortunately Marcos was killed by the men guarding him."

"What happened to Virat and Ramanna?" asked Arya.

"Aisha contacted me after an hour or so as we were packing to be flown to Budapest. What a night that was! I was inches away from being caught, this time being a triple agent to Aisha. Virat and Ramanna followed me when I was on my way, unaware of my followers, to meet her. However, she came prepared. Tanveer was lucky not to be in the scene.

"Virat was of no use to us, and it would have taken us months to crack him, so Ramanna was the obvious choice. Ramanna started talking like a puppet and gave us what we needed – two active agents, their communication protocol and everything, which we used in Budapest. She explained to me, how I should approach this assassination. It was amazing how she planned it; till the last details, like dumping Virat and Ramanna's bodies at the right place to be found after the assassination. She knew all the parties in an out. I projected myself as Virat to RAW, and carried out the task, leaving each and every mark as evidence of RAW work. Then you know the rest…." and that concluded the tale.

"Have you spilled the same to the CIA?" asked Arya.

"Nah… there was no point telling them. These big bullies were just a bunch of chosen pawns. Their sense of superiority would have trashed it completely, right? I kept going with the same tune that I am RAW, and I was just following orders."

Farooq saw the puzzled look on Arya's face.

"I know what you must be thinking. Aisha left me alone to die, then why not save my own skin? She held on to her part of the bargain."

Seeing Arya quiet, he continued talking, "Don't you see the obvious? She always looks so reasonable and projects herself to everyone as if she is always ready to sacrifice herself for you. However, when the time comes, it's always you in the firing line."

It was for the first time Arya saw this old veteran with a different perspective. Somewhere deep down he also sensed her being responsible for his defection.

"I suddenly see a change of heart? Do you regret it?" Arya quizzed.

"No... maybe yes... it doesn't matter now. Good that you are recording it... Must you be?" Farooq's guess was correct. "I am out of options here, Arya. I don't see a bright future outside this cabin."

"Do you want to be saved, Balwinder?" Arya asked.

"Don't call me that!" Farooq's voice had an aggression in it. "All I want is for RAW to learn a lesson, create a manual out of my experience. Don't burn your best in the field just because his hunch went wrong once. I was better during my time; you will soon learn more about me..."

"Farooq, you are still holding on to something..."

Farooq closed his eyes, as if he wanted him to end this episode, and then spoke again, "You are wasting your time on me. She is a ghost. What she did in Budapest was just the first act. The finale is yet to come. You cracked me! Can you crack her? Her first act made everyone believe that RAW is becoming a rouge organization, run by a shrewd set of people, and the second attempt will throw you to the edge of a war, which they are bound to lose. Finding her is the key here, soldier."

The moment those words came out of Farooq's mouth, he saw Arya standing still, eyeballs moving fast, as if he was trying to figure out his next step.

He turned towards the wall; put his leg on the chair adjacent to it and stood up to grab something fixed above.

He came down with a mobile phone. Brigadier was on Skype, video conferencing with Madelyn. It was clear that Arya first connected to Brigadier, then Brigadier further shared this little live feed with Madelyn. With the resources Madelyn had being a CIA, it would have taken just three clicks to find out Arya's location. The fact remained that he was still top priority of the CIA, and the one who snatched Farooq out of their hands. He kept eluding them, and by now, it was all clear that Madelyn and CIA wanted his head. But the way this live feed triangulated from Budapest to India, then further the RAW tech team kept the feed projected from all kinds of phony proxy servers in the world to Madelyn back in Budapest, a highly sophisticated tech team of Madelyn's couldn't do much but to sit and watch this interrogation.

They all waited to start the conversation. Madelyn broke the silence first though, "You've got one hell of an agent, Brigadier." There was a cold glare from Madelyn while looking at Arya on her iPhone. It was the first time she had seen the man.

Arya ignored the praise and focused on the Brigadier before speaking.

"Brigadier, our suspected terrorist Aisha must have gone to Turkey."

"How sure are you?" Madelyn enquired.

"She has lived in Turkey for the last ten years, hiding in plain sight. Therefore, she must have gone back there to erase her existence before opting for a new cover for the next plan. I know one of her accomplices in Turkey. Madelyn, I hope I will not get any roadblocks after this."

"Yes, but until you are accompanied by us."

Arya waited until the Brigadier nodded his approval. "Sure, would love to do a little chit-chat about the weather with you."

"See you at the airport, Madelyn."

Arya closed the session.

Arya looked at the man who claimed to be a remarkable spy once, but now seemed so lost.

The man had sold his soul before, but today his identity as a defector was also taken away. He was a man whom no country wanted. Useless, that's all.

He placed a chair three feet away from Farooq, placing a shining razor blade on that. He looked at Farooq, who also looked at him helplessly.

"You have thirty minutes at the most; choose your options carefully."

Arya moved towards the door, got out of the room and closed the door behind. He never looked back at him, but felt compelled to mutter,

"I therefore commit Farooq to the ground; earth to earth, ashes to ashes, dust to dust; in the sure and certain hope of the Resurrection from his miserable life."

Three

The Red, Trace

O n the way to Turkey, Madelyn spoke smirking, "Strangely…
we found your defector half-dead. He had sliced his own
throat and died bleeding. Like a pig." When she did not get any
response from Arya, she spoke again through clenched teeth.

"Feeling gratified?"

"I just gave him another option; he was smart enough to take
the easier one," Arya spoke without looking at her.

Then, he dialled a number.

The man on the other side of the phone picked up the call
after the eighth ring. Arya could hear the loud noise of sirens.
Must be an ambulance siren, he thought.

"Hello, Tanveer. Arya here. You must have received our
request."

"Yes… I did… But I am afraid I have some bad news for you,
my friend."

He then continued, "Your suspected terrorist came into this
country, removed her known links like Razeeq and a few others.

As they were all found dead with head shots near the Istanbul bazaar. She also made sure that the local media got to the scene first. It delayed police proceedings while she slipped away. I am keeping a tab on every route out of Turkey, but so far nothing to report."

All the passengers on the jet listened to Tanveer; they knew it was not that easy to find her, especially when she was spooked. And her expertise and contacts would never allow her to be found.

Arya replied, "Thank you Tanveer. Would you mind passing all the papers, government documents, video feeds and every document in relation to Mir and his organization to the Indian office?"

Tanveer said, "Okay, but I need clearance approval from my foreign office for that."

Madelyn answered, "Your foreign office has already received the request. It's approved. I appreciate you not to delay this issue. This is Madelyn Hunter from the CIA."

Tanveer was starstruck, and all he could say was, "Sure… it will be shared in ten minutes," before hanging up.

Tanveer never thought that he would see this guy alive again, let alone be accompanied by the CIA. He himself had his share of experiences with the CIA; they dominated this shady world since their existence and always had been the big bullies amongst others.

Arya then said, "Can you reroute this plane to Delhi? There is no point landing in Turkey?"

Matt replied, "Sure," he knew Madelyn would also approve this.

"We need her to be calm. Maddy, could you help me flash some news with my picture?"

"What news?" Maddy, the same denotation again.

The headline in the *The New York Times* dated the 28th September on the front page read:

RAW links tied to the brutal assassination in Budapest.

An Indian shot dead by local authorities while attempting to scrape through the Hungary-Ukrainian border. Evidence confirms that he was a member of the intelligence agency of India, and responsible for the assassinations.

The news article ended with a picture of a dead man.

The same news flashed in all the leading newspapers in the world, and even local reporters followed the same news on their foreign pages.

◆

Indian office of Foreign Affairs, Delhi

"How sure are you that she's read it?" Brigadier said while standing firm on his stance, at the end of that colonial desk. To Arya, the Brigadier looked like a man of composed features, calm, confident but equally ruthless. Jagadish Narayan usually, known with a title 'Brigadier', since he made the toughest of decisions without showing a flicker of doubt.

"Pretty sure. She had a habit of reading the local newspapers everywhere we went," observed Arya.

"Madelyn, our database search has come clean about her image. Nothing on any database, I have pulled all the plugs in the

ISI, Mossad, and MI6 – nothing. All our leads end on this woman, until the point she came into Mir's life in 2004 around March, and as per the Turkish Intelligence, there were scratchy reports that she might have been brought into Turkey illegally. Mir could have brought her in from anywhere in this globe!" Matt looked a bit edgy, being up all night, going through all the files.

"Virat's preliminary report says Mir's organization was found active in Bhutan, Bangladesh, Rawalpindi and Nepal during the 2004 period," Brigadier put a special emphasis on Nepal, which caught Arya's attention.

"Brigadier, did something important happen in Nepal in 2004?"

"Nothing, it's just that the bloody year gave us the unexpected mole."

"Who?" Arya looked around all the parties. Brigadier was silently looking at Madelyn. Matt acted ignorant and Madelyn had a straight face.

"Is there something I should know of?"

"The mole inside RAW, Rabinder, vanished from the face of this earth at the same time and his last whereabouts were in Nepal."

Arya logged in to the RAW database and pulled out all the records related to Rabinder Singh. He went through the files and stopped at Rabinder's last mission. The file didn't have a proper summary of his mission since he vanished midway. It was then that Arya came to know that he was an essential part of the investigation of the 1993 bombings, Parliament attacks and Akshardham attack. All were linked and he was the one to narrow it down to the said Elaf group from Pakistan, who were the mastermind behind all those attacks. This group had their teeth deep inside ISI. What interested him further was that Rabinder was the one who was on that approving panel to give a go head to a black OP to kill all the Elaf group members. When RAW was biting its nails to carry out this stealth mission, no one knew how or why he slipped away to defect with the CIA.

The report also had the detailed description of interview and scrutiny done by RAW once Rabinder was proven to be a defector. Rabinder went to Gangtok along with his deputy, a trip sanctioned by RAW. His deputy Krishna Mohan quoted, "After meeting with his contact, Boss told me that he would wait a bit longer in the city as he needed to check the story through his usual informant." Arya looked at the list of his informants formally enrolled in the RAW database as assets; most of them were hookers from all over India, but none from Sikkim.

Brigadier saw him scanning the files and said with apathetic tone. "There is nothing in there, at least not our terrorist!"

Arya completely ignored him and asked, "I see that while tracing him, we went from Delhi to Sikkim and then to Nepal, where our leads ended."

"Yes, the bastard spent his last days in a beautiful hotel in Gangtok at our expense. Due to security reasons, the hotel had a newly installed camera, which I am sure he didn't know about, otherwise, he wouldn't have left his mark. The video is also there in the bundle report."

Matt stretched his legs on the sofa and yawned, while Madelyn was going through her own daily status reports from European region under her command.

The footage ran through, and both Brigadier and Arya

saw Rabinder coming into the hotel at nine in the evening and checking out fiteen minutes later, paying with the card, and leaving alone.

"I told you…" Brigadier's voice was rather irritated.

"Sir, don't you see the obvious? That man was fooling us the time he checked out, which means he met the one who helped him get away."

He spoke the last few sentences in a very low tone so that only Brigadier who was standing over his shoulders could hear.

Arya saw Madelyn catching snippets of their conversation, but she pretended otherwise.

Arya went through the whole video again; the footage showed this man come into the lobby and sit on a sofa sipping coffee. After forty minutes, he stood up and checked-in. "Nothing out of the ordinary," he murmured.

"We have missed something in these forty minutes…" he stated and again started watching it from the beginning.

On the second run, he zoomed the video to his face, up close, and played it. He watched… waited… and waited… at the thirty-fifth minute, Rabinder took a sip of the coffee. To Arya, it was strange, because he tried to sip coffee out of a mug, which he had already finished a while back. Surely, he was hiding his face from someone, someone he was monitoring or expecting to be there.

Arya enquired furiously, "Do we have any other angle of this hotel?"

Madelyn responded, "Your hunch is baseless here. Why are you digging a grave which is unsubstantial to the case at hand? No wonder whoever he is, he did it right under your nose."

Her words were scathing.

Brigadier tapped his shoulder to calm him down before answering his query. "No, unfortunately not. As I said, they only installed the camera recently and had only one covering the lobby."

Looking at the guest list copy, no one had checked in or checked out with Rabinder. Then he saw that the hotel list had a black mark on room no 56. The room on the same floor where Rabinder stayed. He picked up the phone and dialled the hotel right away, and enquired. The receptionist stated back that she didn't know what he was talking about, and asked for his identity.

"It's a matter of national security. Now do as you're told. Run to whomever you can, but I need to know why your guest list of 15th March 2004 had a black mark against room no 56. You have only fifteen minutes to call me back with this information. Understood?"

As soon as he hung up, he lifted himself from the chair, excused himself with the Brigadier's permission and went to fill up his glass.

"Would you mind? Whatever you're having will do." He heard Madelyn's request to get her a drink as well.

He filled up one for her and handed it over to her. She made a disagreeable face as she took a sip, "Jeez! What is this?"

"It's called Jeepsi... rum. Indian military grade...." He paused for a second and concluded, "Very few have the taste for it." He gulped it all at once and didn't flinch a bit.

Brigadier, who had a little smile peeking from under his thick moustache, saw Madelyn slide her drink aside.

Well, in fifteen minutes, the phone rang and the secretary of the foreign office India, with the permission of the Brigadier, connected the incoming call from the Gangtok hotel.

"Sir, that room was marked black because of the defaulter guest. She didn't check out, nor did she come back to claim her baggage."

"Do you have any sort of identity she submitted at the time of check-in," asked Arya.

"Yes sir, we have a photocopy of the driving license; it's not legitimate though."

"Fax it," responded Arya.

The fax beeped and started printing out the paper. In another thirty seconds, Arya's intuition hit the mark. The black and white picture somewhat resembled Aisha, whose name was Sristi Das on that driving license issued by the Arunachal Pradesh district transport office.

Arya handed over the fax to the Brigadier and asked, "Will you do it, or shall I?" Brigadier nodded and walked around Madelyn's chair.

Brigadier stood glaring out from the window, one hand under his pocket and the other holding his drink, calculated something and came back to her from behind. He whispered something in her ears and then went back to the window again.

Her face was still. She sat for a while, then stood up tapping a sleepy Matt to follow her outside the room.

"She seemed convinced. What was your opening line, Brigadier?"

"I just told her, will you cooperate to get information out from Rabinder, or should I send my new recruit behind him to get it? The choice is yours."

They both shared the same smile. "Cheers!"

◆

A day passed. A meeting took place in one of the meeting chambers of RAW head office in New Delhi.

Arya was asked to be seated as soon as he entered the meeting room. Madelyn, Matt and Brigadier were already present, but this time, there were quite a lot of unknown faces in the meeting as well.

Arya was not formally introduced to them, nor did he want to be.

Brigadier took command and spoke with a confident gesture. "So as per our latest intel, our suspected terrorist, Aisha Bahar, also known to us now as a British national called Anaya McQuillen, was a frequent visitor to India from 1991 till 2004. In this brief time, her whereabouts were mostly found in Arunachal Pradesh. As per our research, she fled the country only five times. As per her visa application and documents, it's known to us now that she entered the country as a correspondent of World News Channel and was tasked to cover a story on Indian tribes. However, she never contacted them back or filed back any story. They did receive her informal resignation, though just a few days after she entered India. As per our sources, her links were attached to Tegi Welfare Society – an NGO presently governed by Rituparna Davidar, a local woman. It's been doing a great deal of work and the Indian government is funding this NGO."

"Who is the source and how sure are we about this information?" One of the bureaucrats broke his silence and interrupted the Brigadier in the middle, by looking at Aisha's projected picture on the screen.

Brigadier replied, "I am sorry, but the source cannot be revealed. In order to get this information, a secrecy act was signed between the Defence Minister of India and the CIA."

The source was the Indian defector Rabinder. Apart from Brigadier and Arya, a few people knew it, such as the Indian Defence Minister and the Prime Minister of India. Madelyn got an unofficial statement from Rabinder, showing her superiors how important his statement would be in order to catch this terrorist. Why did Madelyn go out of her own way? It was a simple and plain fact that Arya still held a trump card over her by the data he had downloaded from the CIA database. Of course, he never officially blackmailed her, but in the world of espionage, you could never be bribed or blackmailed at gunpoint. It's always done on the basis of information. Until now, Arya had not shown any such signs, so she did get the information that was most valuable to Arya at this time in a sense that once he was done with this, she would be able to get the data back.

Brigadier started talking again, as the whispering among the bureaucrats died down.

"Where was I... yes? As per our source, this NGO was a recruiting agency for local tribes into militant organizations known to us as ULFA and the NSCN (K). In January 2010, ULFA softened its stand and has dropped all its demands before the Government of India and NSCN has been neutralized to the extent that it cannot be considered a present threat. However, we all know that these militants are volatile and have been found active forming and supporting a new militant group called ADF. Our sources within BSF and CRPF have confirmed that ADF is now scaling up its activities. The details about the outfit, their sources, and the currently known figures are all in the report you all have in your hands."

The same bureaucrat again interrupted Brigadier. "Then stop the funding. We can't have any links to this NGO. She might use it as an international propaganda to show Indians were involved in her act of terrorism." He looked fit and aged around forty-five. He spoke with a south Indian accent.

"We can't, at least not now. It will spook her and she will never come to us."

"Brigadier, we can't risk getting involved in any international conflict. I am telling you, your job is on the line here."

To these words, the Brigadier smiled while responding, "It's always been on the line, sir… I enjoy being there…"

After a brief pause, the Brigadier spoke again, "I hope you find our reports enough to support the covert mission approved by the defence ministry. As per the request from the ministry, I was filling in all the gaps for you. Do you have any further questions?"

"Not as of now… none," the head bureaucrat spoke and the others nodded.

Brigadier pressed a button on the Cisco phone saying, "Stop the recording."

"If you can excuse us, sir... We have to go into the details of this mission."

They all stood up at once, glared briefly at Madelyn, Brigadier, Matt, and Arya before leaving the room one by one.

Once they left, Brigadier again spoke on the Cisco, "Start the recording for the record operation named *Red Hunt*. It is a joint operation with the Central Intelligence Agency of the United States and RAW's external intelligence agency, DIA."

This operation needed to be jointly carried out by CIA, looking at the involvement of a British national terrorist. Brigadier continued forward with every little detail.

Four

The Red, Martyrs

Somewhere in Arunachal Pradesh district, Changlang forest

Matt and Arya walked to the point they had been instructed to, precisely at noon. They were dressed up as journalists from BBC. A paper note was left for them along with two pieces of a thick cloth, which they were asked to wear on their faces.

They did as told, and waited. They waited for almost four hours before they heard the sound of footsteps on dried leaves. They guessed it to be a four-member team approaching them and they were walking cautiously. A civilian might have missed that faint sound, but it wasn't unheard by Arya. The thick cloth on his face had small gaps enough for him to spot at least one of the men from ADF. The men came near them and waited just to see the two foreign nationals who had approached their leaders to spare some time to be interviewed. Matt and Arya waited and acted as if they didn't even know that they had any company. Arya spoke, "I hate to sit like this Jason, blindfolded!"

"It's okay, don't worry, Sameer," Matt responded to Arya.

The ADF men stayed there silently, for another twenty minutes.

"Hand us all of your electronic items – camera, phone watch – everything!" barked one of the men.

They did as asked.

The men then made a hunting sound, and after a while, a Mahindra jeep came into view. They were asked to sit at the back, and the jeep drove towards the east.

The ride was bumpy for some time, but was smooth as they began to climb up a mountain with sharp turns. They were playing a local song while driving up the hill.

They rode for another thirty minutes, then left the jeep and walked probably three miles on foot. Matt and Arya were still blindfolded and it was getting difficult to walk, so the ADF men chained them with a rope around the waists so that they could sense their way, blindfolded. They denied Arya's request to let them take it off. This was the only way for them to interview the ADF leader. Matt and Arya fell a few times during the narrow walk, but were saved by the ADF men preventing them from sliding down that deadly valley. Arya heard the faint sound of rushing water and estimated they were walking alongside a river. They came close to the same river after a mile until finally they reached the camp.

In the woods, they were asked to be seated on a stool. It was dark when a firm voice spoke in broken English.

"How was your journey to the mountains?"

"Uncomfortable…" Matt responded.

"You asked for it…"

"Yes... I did. Can I take off this shroud?"

"Not until I say so. Tea?"

"Yeah, thank you."

Arya was able to partially look through his blindfold at Matt who was seated right in front of a man. He was asked to be seated away from them.

"Please explain why I should agree to be interviewed by a channel which is pro-Indian?" he began.

"Because I think, your ancestors like the ULFA and others, lacked international recognition. I think any movement such as yours, requires international exposure for your voice to be heard."

Matt stopped. There was no reply from the man. Therefore, he sensed that his offer was hitting its mark.

"At the moment, ADF doesn't exist internationally, and trust me, you will stay that way until you give us your permission. ADF needs a face to be shown and for people to understand your point. The Indian media will not give you that platform which we are capable of providing you."

"I see the questions first, and then I decide if I give the interview."

"We don't do that. You know that we are the highest-rated, most-respected news channels. You know our reputation for integrity and objectivity. We are neither biased to anyone, nor known for tempering our news before the broadcast."

The man didn't speak for a while. Therefore, Matt started again, "Do you wish to be interviewed?"

"Your instructions will reach you. We will start on Wednesday. You will not be carrying anything except your clothes. You will be provided with camera, notepad, and all the recording stuff! Understood?"

"Sure."

The meeting concluded and Arya saw the man leaving, partially through the blindfold.

However, Matt continued, "So where are we staying?"

He soon realized they didn't want them to stay there and that tiring journey back started all over again on the lifeless mountain, at night.

Matt never understood how he managed to walk back through that deadly valley at night. For Arya, it was a gist of his own training with the army.

Then the tiring visits started almost every day. Matt and Arya posed as Jason and Sameer, started mixing with the young cadres and through the process of interview, understood how they were misled to fight against their own country. Every meeting took place in the different hills of Arunachal Pradesh and every day they climbed up through different routes. The ADF was newborn, bred by militants, but their acts were thorough, professional and they always strip-searched Matt and Arya. Every act of the ADF men concluded that they were very hard-headed and rigid. Arya and Matt were not moving ahead even after four such meetings. The ADF was not giving out anything except for their motives and adjectives. Arya soon came to realize that the ADF needed to be infiltrated deep inside as soon as possible. Brigadier accordingly agreed, and soon, a second phase of the plan was crafted for Arya.

In their next meeting, Matt threw a strategic question to the ADF commander.

"How do you plan to deal with the military elite specialist team known as the Black Face?"

To his question, the commander appeared clueless and showed a worried face.

Matt showed him substantial proof that indeed a military force had been formed to deal with militants, which had been named Black Face. This team had been very successful wherever they went and was now headed to Arunachal Pradesh.

The commander looked worried, but said that they were ready for any such team. Meanwhile, Arya was strategically taking pictures and keeping an eye on the interview.

All of a sudden, few well-built men came out from the bushes and stood in front. All of them were dressed like local villagers but their appearances seemed otherwise. Everyone was stunned; the ADF men looked panicked and drew their guns at them. Matt and Arya were standing along with the ADF men and the villagers were facing them ten feet away.

One of the ADF men moved towards the villagers and asked something in the local language, but he didn't get an answer. Instead, a bullet thrashed his skull and a shocked moment passed as they looked and watched each other.

The villagers drew their guns and the bullets started firing all around. The villagers were experts and killed five before they could get to their preferred cover. The villagers had a sniper somewhere dead straight, providing enough support. The ADF was trapped from all sides; no one could move an inch. There could be a chance that the villagers might misfire, but the sniper would not miss for sure. There was chaos and one of the ADF men then grabbed Matt and came forward hiding behind him.

Looking at the foreign figure, the shooting stopped for a while, Matt spoke furiously, "I am from the BBC… don't shoot… don't shoot! I am from the press."

However, the men posing as villagers were in no mood to stop anyway.

One of them shot Matt in the leg, and as Matt fell down, the second one took a head shot at that ADF man. His body dropped lifeless in seconds. Now only three men were left from the ADF side, along with Arya. They all saw their end in each other's eyes.

One of the AK47 was lying at Arya's feet; he grabbed it and started firing like a maniac. He cried out aloud, "You bastards!" looking at Matt bleeding.

All the rounds went here and there. He emptied his round all at once and there was silence all around when suddenly two bodies dropped like a dead leaf from behind one of the trees. Those two men posing as villagers were not so lucky, it seemed.

As soon as his round finished, he grabbed another AK47 lying on the ground and started firing again, the villagers now feared for their lives and ran to get more cover.

The commander took this opportunity to escape. He came from behind and grabbed Arya, snatched him from the scene and ran, dragging him along with the other one left. However, Arya was still firing his last round randomly.

Matt looked up from the ground at one of the villagers and smiled.

Their plan had worked; he stayed on the ground and signalled to all the men posing as villagers to stay where they were.

The ADF commander and his only left comrade were very swift; they covered a distance of three miles in a few minutes, dragging Arya along with them. The commander saw this guy as a saviour and knew there wouldn't be any place left for him in this bloody contemptuous world after what he had done to those villagers – 'Black Face'.

To the commander, this guy Sameer was just as unfortunate as the commander himself, and the only place left for him to survive were these far-reaching woods. There was a point from where they could see the spot where the shooting had taken place. The commander and his comrade looked through their binoculars to see if they were being pursued by the army. They were not being followed, but through the binoculars they saw the Black Face team burying the dead bodies of the ADF men, along with the BBC reporter. The commander felt his rage boiling as the government now took the route of erasing their identities itself. No report, no bodies, no news. A black ops team way to finish off separators like ADF. The comrade then showed some doubt and spoke to his commander in the local language, "How did the army find out about the place?"

They looked back at the man who was now in a situation of belonging to no man's land. Sameer looked lost and was seated idly, where he was asked to sit. The commander walked up to the nearby small cave fit for a small animal like jackals. There were few fresh patches of green grass resembling sea fungus. He cut out a few of those from the cave wall and pressed it into his mouth. It had enough moisture to satisfy his dry throat. He then rubbed it on his face and neck. He offered Sameer some of it and helped him to drink it too.

"Did you notice someone following you around in the city where you have been living?"

"No! No! Why would anyone follow us? "

"To get to us… Sorry, my friend, but can you bear with me? I need to strip search you once again."

Arya didn't object; he was clean and had nothing on him.

The comrade concluded it must have been Jason, otherwise there was no way they could have found them deep in the forest.

Arya was standing naked, his palms covering his private parts, and his face down with embarrassment. The commander gave him back his clothes and then Arya spoke hesitantly, "Commander, could we stay here a bit longer?"

"Why?"

"I feel… I mean I need to… to go to the toilet!"

Commander said, "Go over to the bushes and hurry up! We need to move ahead."

The commander was amused; he himself has been thinking along the same lines.

In the bushes, Arya fought hard and felt immense pain, but managed to get the tracker, the size of a lollipop, out of his ass. The ADF men had a scanner, which could detect any transmitting device, even if it was transplanted inside your flesh, so Arya had to shove a tracker up his ass with a thread connected to it, with a tiny bit left outside, which he used now to pull it out. If the transmitter was switched off, then it couldn't be detected. Arya had to start sending signals, because it had been forty-five minutes since he was off the grid with the ADF men. The moment it was switched on, on the other side of the woods, the Brigadier came out of the van, knowing his agent was alive and on to his mission.

Arya, along with the Commander and a comrade, reached the ADF base at midnight. The commander took the longer, more difficult route to reach his base. What he didn't know was now the army didn't need to tail them anymore.

The days went by and Arya never looked comfortable in the woods to any of the ADF men. They usually laughed at his back. Looking at how he struggled daily with the mosquitoes, hated going to relieve himself in the open and eating *tama*. Tama was soft and potato-like which was extracted out of a certain plant. It was tasteless, raw and had a sandy feel to it. He was considered as a good for nothing man. He was assigned to do certain tasks, like getting water for all of the ADF men, cleaning and odd jobs like that, but was never left alone. A thirteen-year-old village boy always accompanied him. This young boy didn't have much of his own understanding, but was sure that he wanted be a comrade.

During the following month, Arya saw the ADF men going somewhere and returning with supplies and other necessary materials. He noticed that a group of ADF men were being trained in hand to hand combat with knives and other sharp objects. Their routine training always had two hours of technical briefing session, at least on some days, Arya thought. A man visited the camp daily, trained them and left. After a few days, Arya understood that the man was a trainer of some foreign language. As the day progressed, Arya confirmed that all twenty comrades were of the same ethnicity – Bo'gaer – a section of the Lhoba ethnic group, long residing in the northeastern region of India. The two main tribal groups, which fall under the designation 'Lhoba' in Tibet are the Yidu (Idu Mishmi) and the Bo'gaer (Bokar Adi), who were found in far greater numbers inside Arunachal Pradesh, a state of modern-day India that was now proudly claimed by China. These ADF comrades may have come into India a long time ago, leaving their family in COA (China occupied Arunachal Pradesh).

These ADF men were not a major threat to India, if given proper sanctions. It was just a matter of days for the Indian Army to clean up these radicals, but you know how active politics goes around, using these militants as a reason to draw the voters of the state. Therefore, the Indian Army never got the approval for such a full-scale operation. For Arya, capturing the woman was the main reason for being here, and he could sense it was all a matter of time when his wait would be over. So he kept his mind cool, and arranged all the necessary communication channels. Within a few days of his suspicion, he set up an encrypted communication protocol with the Brigadier and the team. By then, Arya had created enough ease around the camp, so no one suspected him roaming around here and there with his best pal, the thirteen-year-old boy, and collecting rubbish. The boy was the only one who saw Arya making those listening devices with paper cups and wooden sticks, a few batteries and stuff like that, which was scrap for others.

Technology is making communication easy these days, but it makes information more vulnerable. For example, bluetooth on a cell phone is an easy way to send information wirelessly over a short distance. You get an antenna and you can use the bluetooth from someone's phone to send the same information over a long distance. An antenna looks tricky, but given a few hours of expert training, you can do it in a matter of minutes. A paper can, along with some metal chips, can be a cute little antenna connected to a stolen USB cable to connect it with a high-frequency tracker. Then you could send a coded message through the commander's phone using his bluetooth. The young boy looked amazed at how his new friend used to give him time to play with some toys with a sworn promise that no one would know about their secret affair.

From that day on, the Brigadier, with the CRPF and the Army, was on standby for a full-fledged infiltration. Brigadier, on the other hand, kept a very tight leash on any speculation going about the covert op. He knew that even though the ruling government on a central level had approved it, any wind of this on the opposition side could side-track this op.

Arya later gathered and communicated to his base that the comrades would soon get permission to proceed.

Five

The Red, Resurrection

It was a usual day in the ADF camp, nothing extraordinary. Arya sent the signals to Brigadier that the ADF men had come back with their routine supplies. The Brigadier responded that nothing out of the ordinary had happened during the supplies exchange in the city.

The days sped by. Six months had passed in the camp. Arya's hunch had not paid off. He knew RAW with CIA had exhausted their resources to trace her, but every dot had ended without connecting it to her. This well-crafted, beautiful, wicked bitch had always been a myth to him; he could never get out those beautiful, pleasant memories of her being a perfect partner from his head. She had always been a survivor, a tantalizingly seductive and a sharp one. Madelyn withdrew her position a few days ago, assured that the target they were after was not coming back. Arya had reflected the same in his earlier communication. He saw the ADF men being restless for the past few weeks. Arya overheard the commander expressing his concerns that they were being delayed, and were behind their schedule. Arya didn't know what step to take next.

The Brigadier ordered him to stay put for another month before he could launch an attack on the ADF base.

She was never coming back, he concluded before shutting his eyes for a nap.

It was about three in the morning when Arya heard the sound of a vehicle. He woke up, and hurriedly got out of his bed to see through a small hole in his tent. Something had happened, something in those two hours of his sleep. He came out of his tent at once, only to receive a deadly blow on his temple from the wooden handle of a rifle. The blow was so powerful that no sound came from him.

The next thing he knew, someone was splashing water on his face. It took him some seconds to understand that he was hanging from a tree, upside down, and his hands were tied at the back. He looked down at all those ADF men hurriedly wrapping up their things. They looked like ants as he was still recovering from that blow on the temple. He couldn't understand how they had found out his identity, or else he wouldn't have got such a treatment. He bided his time, but couldn't make out much. In a matter of minutes, the whole camp had vanished as he hung there. He watched and calculated that ten out of the twenty comrades boarded the jeep and drove off from the scene. He wanted to send the distress signal, but his tracker was not in his possession. Soon after everything was wrapped up, the early morning sunshine reached the ADF camp. At that moment, the commander gave the final orders to the remaining ADF men and soon they too fled the scene. The commander came close to Arya, drawing out his razor-sharp kukri. It was only a matter of time, when he'd finally use it to behead Arya and leave him hanging from the tree.

A female voice called off this execution, and when the commander stepped aside, Arya saw that very beautiful evil being walking towards him wearing a black outfit. Lighting a cigarette, she herself looked like a comrade, but surely, she was their leader – Aisha… Anaya… Noori – call her whatever you like. Her every step towards Arya showed how proud, how arrogant she was, and also how evil.

She came close to him, touched his lips for a while and gave him a pleasant smile. The next thing he knew, she drew out her gun and with a single shot, cut the rope tying him to the tree, making him drop to the ground. Arya managed not to fall on the ground with this head first, but then there was a clear sound of his shoulder bone crunching as he fell with his whole weight on his right side. He had sorely misplaced his shoulder bone. He grunted again before managing to get himself on to his knees.

"Cigarette?"

"I am thinking of quitting!" Arya replied while attempting to straighten his shoulder, trying to assesses if it was broken.

"You shouldn't have ditched me, Mr Spook. We would have made a great team together."

"Well, if you had levelled with me earlier, I might have had different plans for you."

"And what would that be… an apology letter from your Chief?"

"No, a plain and simple headshot to rest your soul and then I might have attended your lone funeral too."

She giggled. "Oh! You're such darling!" She looked at the time.

One of the ADF men brought out all the gadgets which they had found while searching Arya's tent.

She picked up the pieces and sent a single. Strangely, she knew the exact protocol to communicate with Arya's team.

While finishing, she said, "Here you go… your Brigadier and the team has been updated that everything is fine."

"Don't worry, I will not give you such an easy way out."

She took her chair and started counting her steps backwards. At that moment, she overheard her captive's exhausted words. "Why?"

However, she continued until she counted the twentieth step. She placed her chair to settle herself on it.

"RAW destroyed me, my family. My father was sent home barely alive. You know all that, right? I mean, what do you expect me to do, after all that hospitality you Indians served?"

He drew his chin up, looked her in the eye. "I want real answers. I am sure this wasn't just revenge for your father? I mean, if I understand your astonishing career, you are not that type."

"What's my type then?"

"Do you desire to switch seats with me?"

"Hahaha… I love it when you are frustrated. Do you want me to confess?"

She had a scary laugh before her eyes turned into stone. "That's my secret…. It will live and die with me."

"Cut him loose…" she told the commander.

"Let's see how your comrades are up to the task, commander! Show me if they have any genocidal instinct? Also, my darling, let's see if you are as good as your files say you are?"

That last sentence was Arya's death warrant.

There was nothing left now for any sort of negotiation. It was clear that she wanted to have fun before finally killing him.

Arya stood up and saw the ADF men lining up in 2/2 formation till the end. These were a second lot of the comrades trained in the camp. The second batch of hers to execute a different plan probably. The first lot was already on the move somewhere in the jungle, and at the end of them, there was the commander. The ADF men had equally dead faces. They looked like unleashed sled dogs accompanied by their choice of weapon – the kukri, butcher knife, hammer, hatchet, among others.

They all were taking calm and short breaths, whereas Arya was not given any choice of weapon. Arya looked at each of them one by one, with their weapons. The first two had small knives in their hands. In such a situation, you are bound to get hit by your trained enemy, but what best you can do is to not get cut in vulnerable places. Speed is your only weapon. Arya had that.

The first ADF man ran towards him, wildly screaming, and started swinging the knife across. Arya survived it by ducking at the right time and grabbing his fist, twisting it towards his abdomen and drawing him close. Grabbing his shoulder, he forced the guy's own knife to dig deeper into his abdomen. A clear clinching sound arose as the knife went deeper and deeper inside, drawing a disgruntled noise. First, he vomited blood and then thrashed about. Nine left out of ten, but now

Arya had a knife shining in his right hand. The ADF men had always seen him as a hopeless guy since he had arrived in the camp. A good for nothing. But this new avatar made them think otherwise.

Two comrades ran towards him. Arya took a deep breath and chose the right one to attack first. He had a hatchet. It was a great weapon, but needed to be manoeuvred correctly. Arya too took three steps towards the right one and kicked the left one in the jaw, sending him away. He jabbed the first swing, ducked down and cut him in the ankle, along with a blow to his kneecap and on his chest. Enough to freeze his brain.

A large kitchen knife grazed his left arm and made a clean cut. Another comrade was back in his position just behind the comrade in Arya's grip. Arya knew this would happen, but didn't care for the cut. This was the one basic difference between Arya and the ADF men. He was more mentally prepared to die. The fight between Arya and the ADF comrades carried on for quite a while and it was violent, as Arya beat them single-handedly.

There was a pause for a moment when everyone tried to make sense of what was happening. A laugh made them realize there was an evil soul enjoying every bit of this deadly fight. Her appreciation made Arya mad with fury and understanding, that she was making him kill his own compatriots. Arya pushed the dead fourth comrade aside as he was not a great shield anymore. The third one was the nearest one to grab and he jabbed him with the knife. The third one dropped like a dead leaf. During this time, the seventh one somehow managed to make two nasty cuts on the back of his spinal cord, making him lose the sensation of his legs. Arya trembled and saw no easy way out of this mess.

By now, the ADF comrades had joined the fight, fearing that just one of them couldn't kill him, not alone. There was a huge stone on which Arya rested his back while holding one of them in his possession. He watched all the ADF men moving towards him rapidly – the seventh, eighth, ninth, tenth and the second one.

Arya had to do something drastic.

He started dragging the sixth one away as the ADF men searched for a place to get near him. He then started inflicting wounds on the sixth comrade's wrist, every cut was wild and made the sixth one cry aloud for mercy, but he didn't stop. He was still dragging him away, wounding him. All the ADF men helplessly watched him and suddenly all of them stopped following him. Arya knew he had made them vulnerable enough to think what their end might be like.

He looked at all of them and screamed, *"Back off! Now! Run away while you can!"* His eyes were red and his whole face was smeared with blood, as the sixth one was still crying for mercy. The ADF men kept watching. They were rooted to their spot and were hesitant to step ahead, as one of them remembered sharing a meal with this beast once.

Arya watched for another second and when the ADF men didn't turn away, he took this brutality to the next level. The crying sixth comrade received two fatal blows, ending his life, Arya then drew out the knife from his heart and a spray of blood made it look like a small fountain gushing out onto his face. He then carried out more gruesome acts which stunned the ADF men. Nobody enjoyed it other than the devil herself; her face displayed a wicked smile.

The commander, on the other hand, did some soul searching and fled the scene. He ran towards the woods. He knew he didn't have a chance, so he took the necessary step for survival. But before he could complete ten yards, a bullet thrashed his skull and he dropped to the ground, lifeless.

Aisha curtsied, and then shot him dead.

The rest of the ADF men knew they couldn't run away like their commander, so the only option left was to try and kill this man-eater.

The seventh one ran towards Arya, screaming.

Arya was ready again this time again, defeating all, until the ninth one twisted around and wounded him with a dagger. One of them managed to hit him at last. He dropped his knife from one hand, picked it up with the other and made a wound in the ninth comrade's leg. Before anyone could hit any other fatal blow, he stood up fast and went behind him. Arya fixed his knife around his neck, looked at the ones left in front of him. Then punched full blows to the chest of the ninth comrade. The eighth one ran furiously towards him while the tenth one just stood still.

The eighth one tried, but Arya never let the man understand how he had grabbed his wrist forcing his arm around and pushing him to the ground facing his front before twisting his arm clockwise then vice versa thus breaking his bones. A final punch on his spinal cord at the edge of his neck made him die instantly.

The tenth one dropped his hammer on the ground, when he saw this hunter run towards him.

However, before Arya could reach him and slice him up, he dropped dead as he was shot from the back.

Arya looked around at the bloody mess. Few of the men were still bleeding, coughing out blood. Aisha fired one shot after another and killed each ADF, while Arya stood in the middle of the red soil.

She had a perfect smile, as always. "You know, your files say you could handle seven men at a time in hand to hand combat. You superseded your own reputation here, my love."

Arya looked at her posture. He had waited for this moment for quite a while. There were a thousand questions running through his head. She was not remotely the same Aisha, for whom Arya had once felt something special. He fiddled around with his own conscience. Was it the Aisha he met in Turkey or was she a myth, or the devil himself?

She tossed her gun away and drew out a small knife with a handle specially designed. It had a curved edge. It made a whistling sound as she drew it out in the air. It sure looked like a Korean piece. Arya was tired, his shoulders slouched, but his eyes were burning red. She moved towards him at full speed.

Arya stood right there and waited for her to reach him. This fight was different. It was not to save the country or anyone. This fight was purely personal, between two of them, whose path had crossed while achieving their motives. This was not for any greater good or bad. Between them, this fight was to finish the other one and to end this tiring chase.

The first swing from Aisha's knife made a neat sound while passing through Arya. He was just inches away from it, her knife's curvy edge was meant to slash anything in its way. And so it did to Arya's jacket. It was sliced open, but the other two of her swings didn't miss the flesh, though the cuts were not deep. As if she didn't want him to die like this. Arya was tired enough, so he didn't manage to save himself, or he intentionally accepted those wounds. He took a swing with his fist, which didn't hit her. He turned towards her again and took another shot. She was nearly four feet away from him, ready. At that moment, Arya felt a terrible burning sensation on the cuts she had made. It was acidic. He froze for a moment as he felt a little disconnected from his own senses.

"Ah…." he grunted while looking at the cut.

The parts where she had made the cuts were not losing blood; they had turned green. Arya realized that her knife must have been dipped in some kind of poison. He was raging with anger while she stood there, laughing at him. He trembled but moved towards her; she moved back, signalling him to catch up with her. He knew he was beaten by her screwed immoral mind. When she pretended to have a fair fight throwing her gun away, the thought didn't even occur in his mind that she was smart enough to know that she couldn't beat him with a straight arrow. He certainly forgot the most basic lesson of his training – don't waste your energy abhorring your enemy; it clouds your judgment.

At this point, his throat had a sandpaper feel, and moments later, he felt his lungs desperately trying to grasp air. His whole body started to crumble and shake hysterically. He didn't notice, but he was on the ground while Aisha came near him and touched his face. The veins on his forehead turned green.

"This is just the beginning, my love; don't fight it. No one survived…" "You are among the few men I have enjoyed the most. If it was any consolation, I might consider it while killing you finally."

These last words resonated with him before Arya started losing his consciousness gradually. Lying on the ground, he heard a footfall approaching silently towards them. He only saw a booted leg approaching Aisha from behind. Whoever it was knew how to walk dead silently on dry land with dead leaves strewn over it. Arya also might not have noticed the silent footsteps if his ears had not been in contact with the ground.

Six

The Red, Guardian

Arya got back some of his senses. He didn't have enough energy to open his eyes. His hands shook at first, then his toes – the first of the many senses he felt as the rain hit his numb body. His fists were burning and he felt a pinching sensation in his wrists as if attached to an intravenous. After few brief gulps of saliva, he finally managed to open his eyes. He found himself under a large peepal tree. The rainfall was falling hard and that gave him a blurry vision. His blurry vision made out a few corpses lying a few feet away. Arya's conscience snapped, realizing Aisha had poisoned him. And as soon as he realized this, he heard someone choking and coughing at a distance. He wanted to clear his vision, but the raindrops were too heavy for him to see clearly along with the poison affecting his body. He then heard the sound of metal, as if someone was beating someone deliberately and rapidly in the distance. He realized there was a man in a green T-shirt, hunter trousers and jungle boots – the same booted man, and he was pounding Aisha with a metal rod. She was hung upside down a few metres away; her face covered with a see-through plastic bag filled with water, perhaps. She was choking as well as getting the third-degree treatment.

Who was this man? A thought echoed inside Arya.

The man then cut the plastic bag open. Arya noticed Aisha gasping for breath. When the mysterious man realized Arya was watching him, he deliberately turned his head away. The mysterious man turned towards him after hiding his face behind a Velcro mask. He wore an Army cap before walking towards Arya, giving Aisha some rest.

Arya was still in immense pain, and even after a lot of effort, he couldn't move either his legs or his hands. The unknown man sat down on his knees and checked Arya's poisonous wounds. He changed the empty saline drip with a new one. He injected it with a couple of drops of some unknown liquid. The man surely knew what he was doing, but who was he? Another DIA? Someone from RAW? An Army personnel or a guardian angel? Arya felt a wave of dizziness again; his eyes went heavy. He tried to speak up, but in turn, he only managed to murmur in a broken tone, "I want… want… she is mine…"

The unknown man placed his hand on Arya's shoulder and tapped him, saying, "You did great, Rangroot! Hold your guard. I will not let you die like this; bear with me for some time. She poisoned you with some variation of TTX, and it's a potent neurotoxin. Remember that…!"

The dizziness caused by the saline pushed Arya into another spell of deep sleep.

He saw the unknown man walking up to Aisha, and before Arya lost his full consciousness, her deadly screams echoed in the heavy rain. She seemed fearful of this unknown man approaching her bit by bit and tried very unsuccessfully to free herself. Arya's eyes closed and he got swallowed by a dark hole.

Roughly around 9 a.m. in the woods, the unknown man broke a small vial filled with a liquid and kept it near Arya. Arya woke up at once with the fumes hitting his nostrils; it took him merely half a second to come back to his full senses when he saw the unknown man walking away.

"Stop…" he shouted. "Who are you?"

The man stopped and said, "You don't want to know, and it's for your own good."

He said those words and ran away in the woods like a cheetah. He was unbelievably fast, considering his age.

In the adrenal rush of such a situation, you tend to miss the minor details, details that look obvious but make a lot of significance. Arya sensed that the unknown man was in his fifties due to the shrivelled skin of his hand. He was in possession of a Tanfoglio T95, an Italian impressive piece of 9mm. Apart from this, Arya couldn't gather much. He looked firm, he was medium built, but his fist felt firmer and heavier. This man didn't give away any leads, and suddenly Arya remembered those deep eyes of his mysterious saviour. He had tired red eyes, as if Arya has always known those eyes. But when and where was the real question.

The clandestine man was a professional. No wonder he broke Aisha in a matter of hours while no one else could.

Thinking of Aisha made him curious about her, and he turned to look at the other side.

A gasp came out of his mouth. He couldn't believe what that man had done to her. Arya tried to stand, but fumbled on his feet;

the poison still bothered him. His left leg was still numb and at first, he felt paralyzed. He limped when he walked towards the dead corpse of Aisha, still hanging upside down. Her decaying body swollen and foul smelling. The stink was so thick and rich that he could almost taste it.

He threw up suddenly, and his abdomen rumbled inside. He knew he would never get the smell of her burning flesh out of his mind. No matter how long he lived.

He examined her corpse, her own Korean knife was thrust half inside her neck. She had been tortured first and when the time came, he had slit her throat open, letting her bleed. A 'halal'.

The soil beneath her was covered with fresh blood slowly turning black, with bees humming around it. It was evidently revenge. Looking at the position of the corpse, it was clear that she had been burnt alive. There was no substance or fuel of any inflammable element evident, so it was also clear that she was burnt slowly in her own body fat. This corpse looked so ugly that no one would believe that it belonged to one of the most beautiful women he had ever met. The burnt corpse pleased Arya. He knew it shouldn't, but it did.

Next to her on the stool was a mobile phone with a piece of paper stuck underneath. The wind after the rain was calm, but the paper was fluttering in the wind. He walked up to it:

The more calmly you kill your nemesis, the calmer you will feel for the rest of your life. Understand that you are not a murderer by nature; you kill someone for your duty, for your country. Everything that you need is on the phone. I will leave you with it. How you use it, is up to you.

You are on the clock; her comrades are on their way and you are six hours behind. They are heading for Tibet, then to China. If you hurry, you can still get them before crossing the border. They might be found on the mountain range, three clicks north of the Dibang Wildlife Sanctuary. I hope you will never need me again. Don't try to follow me; it's useless.

The unknown man was indeed a guardian, probably a sleeper. Arya buried Aisha in the woods, and indeed, he was the lone attendant at her funeral.

"I, therefore, commit Aisha to the ground. Earth to earth, ashes to ashes, dust to dust; in the sure and certain hope of resurrection from her wretched life."

Arya never understood why he said those words to Aisha while cremating her. Maybe somewhere deep down, he understood her motive was driven by the actions of his own countrymen, responsible for making her what she was.

Arya briefed Brigadier about the status, who then coordinated with the BSF commander to catch those ten men heading for Tibet. He took the long walk to the base. During the journey, he listened to two sets of the interrogation audio. She elucidated her entire journey in the first, her assets and other essential details of her planning to crucify RAW. After several attempts, she never could really explain how a covert mission details landed on her lap. All she knew was that Mir had some secret friend in the ISI, who knew the profiles of the RAW elite team, tasked to eliminate Mir. When she got wind of it, she saw her chance. The chance she was waiting for since 2004, with her own resources either burnt or dead, like Shariff, and she was no more than a slut to Mir. She had waited for such chance and when the day came, she used Mir's shadow and his resources to achieve her motives. Even Mir was unaware of her actual motives; to her, Mir was just a tool, used in a precise manner. Her timings were impeccable, and she always had been in contact with the NGO she had formed in India.

In the second set, the mystery man asked the most devious question of all.

What do you know about 'Changez'?

Arya's weary eyes showed alertness, sensing he might get some answers to the question he himself had already been interrogated about before.

She only remembered Mir and his ISI contact discussing the name 'Changez' when the ISI men specifically instructed Mir to gather any information about an Operation Changez and the length of RAW's understanding of it.

At this point, he noticed that the mystery man was very conscious of not being seen in the video while ending the interrogation. And then Arya remembered something... Something that the man had said to him while treating him. A word, which was probably the only mistake the mysterious man made, or was it deliberate?

Victoria House, RAW Safe House
Chowringhee Square, Kolkata
The next day, 9 a.m. local time

Red tape recording session:

Abhimanyu explained his side of the story, starting from the day he reached Izmir, Turkey, from the death of the operative Zehana, to his encounter with the CIA, his time in Budapest, leaving the part that he still held data that belonged to the CIA, and understanding about the terrorist Aisha Bahar a.k.a Anaya McQuillen a.k.a Noori Agah Khan Niazi.

When he was asked, "Your feelings towards Aisha? And why you chose to kill her?"

"My actions were self-explanatory; she was of no use to us." Abhimanyu showed zero emotions, his pulse showed normal to the lie detector machine strapped to his wrist and chest. Everyone who saw that video took it for a granted that the man interrogating Aisha was Abhimanyu. He never gave a straight answer about where he exactly buried her corpse while emphasizing the truth. Brigadier interrupted the interrogator and requested him to skip that part.

The session ended by giving a code name to the mission as 'Red Hunt', and that was the last sign of her in the files of the RAW database as 'The Red'.

Abhimanyu kept the mysterious man's identity to himself. By now, he had a fair idea about why the mystery man chose to record the most important question in the second video session about Changez.

There was a mole deep inside RAW. The mystery man became even more mysterious for Abhimanyu. Although he was asked not to follow up, Abhimanyu was always a loose cannon when it came to following orders. He not only wanted to understand why the mystery man came to save him, he also wanted to know the real picture. There was something going on inside RAW.

Two days after the red tape session

A steady but an unpredictable change in weather took place when a cyclone hit Kolkata. In a matter of hours, the sky opened up, making the lives of the residents miserable. The day was dark, cold and dreary. It really couldn't get any worse. The city of joy was accustomed to regular evening showers with the sun playing hide and seek in the clouds, but this was not just any other day. The weather had changed drastically in the last twenty-four hours. One could easily see the difference of the two worlds. One created by men who loathed the sight of mud on the sidewalk formed by the clogged drainage system, which obviously wasn't potent enough to handle such rain. The motorists loathed the sight of the pedestrians walking down the motorway, because apparently, the sidewalk wasn't good enough for them. The lone traffic controller loathed the sight of honking motorists and yelling pedestrians. It was a world of loathing. Then there was another world created by the gods. A world ruled by Mother Nature.

The deluge situation got better as Abhimanyu reached the other part of the city – New Town, a neighbourhood of Kolkata. This newly developed, fast-growing, planned satellite city being developed mainly for information technology and also as a residential hub on the north-eastern fringes of the city. The cyclone had made New Town resemble a wet desert. Abhimanyu couldn't find a soul when he got off the local yellow cab. He moved towards the single apartment, he knew, his mystery man possessed in this part of the city. He wanted a resolution to all those questions swarming in his mind. His curiosity grew as he walked towards the only house sitting on the lane bisecting at regular intervals in-between the vacant plots. The single two-storey house was easy to spot from the major arterial road on its south side, and the walk took him roughly fifteen minutes. At the door, he listened for a moment. After a few minutes, he was satisfied that there was no suspicious activity in front of the building, no idling car, no loitering pedestrians.

He knocked.

No answer. It had taken him two days to get the exact location of this mystery man, Shubhendu Sarkar. The man who had trained him, mentored him, and at last, protected him.

He knocked again. "Shubhendu?" A few more minutes went by, and no answer.

He scanned the surroundings again, before taking out a jack-knife style lock pick with tempered stainless steel picks, knurled stainless steel set screw for a positive lockup, and a hard alloy handle. He picked one of six steel intact in this set to open the door with a slight jig and the door lock gave away. The door opened, and Abhimanyu carefully entered. The lights were switched off in the lower part of the house, which had a dining area, kitchen, and a single sofa. The place was damp and dusty. There was a staircase on the left side, with a dim light emanating from the upper part of the house. He reached upstairs; it had a single room with a dim light. The door was half-open, and as soon as he entered calling out, "Shubhendu", his fear turned into reality.

Shubhendu lay on his back on the floor next to the study table with a laptop. Shubhendu's face had turned purple, and his eyes were bulging out horribly. His tongue was half out, clinched in-between his teeth, and limped outside. Abhimanyu dropped to the floor, and couldn't help sobbing. There was a thin, deep reddish line, damaging his haemorrhaged tissue. His mentor had been murdered.

"Who did this?" Abhimanyu said in a low but ferocious voice. "Who the hell did this to you?"

Spies do hunt other spies in the field; it's a necessity of the job. However, this was murder – a murder to make a statement. The murderer seemed to relish the method. Then how can a man like Shubhendu, a master in the game of espionage, be so careless for his nemesis to come and capture him? The thought stunned Abhimanyu. At that point, he noticed a couple of glasses placed on the reading table alongside the laptop.

One of the chairs was upside down, giving a hint of Shubhendu's resistance to that deadly trap, his struggle to survive. First glass was empty, presumably Shubhendu's, and on the other side desk was another glass filled with Scotch, left untouched. The crime scene started to make sense. Whoever killed Shubhendu was someone he trusted. To be precise, a friend. Shubhendu let his killer walk into the house, and even offered him a drink. He was betrayed, betrayed by someone who pretended to be a friend.

Shubhendu was killed by one of us! were the last thoughts as Abhimanyu left the scene.

Epilogue

Club Faru, Maldives

A tall broad man sat on a beach chair reading an article on his iPad. The private beach was silent. Crashing against the shore, small waves kissed the unscathed white sand set as far as his eyes could see. A gentle sea breeze rustled through his grey hair. He was an older man, in his early fifties. He could taste the salt in the air because it was so strong. For a moment, the beauty of the island distracted him. The sound of the water against the shore, and the jazz music being played at the beach shop grilling lobsters and all kinds of seafood.

The article he was reading, read:

The news came in live from the Chinese city of Kunming, Yunnan, on 1 March 2014. The earlier BBC reports suggest that, at around 9:20 pm local time, a group of eight knife-wielding men and women attacked passengers at the city's railway station. Both male and female attackers were seen pulling out long-bladed knives and proceeded to stab and slash passengers. At the scene, police killed four assailants and captured one injured female.

No group or individual stepped forward to claim responsibility for the attack. However, the local news channel Xinhua News Agency announced within hours of the incident that the separatist Uyghur carried it out. The government officials in Kunming are yet to comment on this.

The beer next to him was warmer than he would have preferred, but he didn't care. The article, which had his full attention, did not give the results he had planned. The man was deep in his thoughts when his phone vibrated. As he picked it up, a familiar voice spoke over the phone.

"We have failed, you failed!" in a harsh tone.

"If your girl can't kill a bloody rookie, we are better off without her. You can't pin this on me."

"Oh, is that's so? Don't you dare play a game with me. I sense, your rookie had some help. There was no chance of our failure; he did everything under your nose, and the irony was, you helped him."

"So what do you suggest? What could I have done to stop him? Kill him point blank and incarcerate myself?"

"Is your cover still intact? Be precise."

"Of course it is. I have given my entire life for this cover. I have killed too many friends to save this cover, so don't give me that attitude. I know what I am doing."

There was a long silence then, when the man on the other side enquired, "Are you there?"

"Yes, it's about time," he said his words carefully while speaking.

"Time? Time for what?" said the man over the phone.

"To activate Changez."

List of Acronyms

ADF	–	Allied Democratic Forces
BBC	–	British Broadcasting Corporation
BSF	–	Border Security Force
CIA	–	Central Intelligence Agency
CIT X/ CIT J	–	Counterintelligence Team of RAW for Pakistan and Khalistan
COA	–	China Occupied Arunachal Pradesh
CRPF	–	Central Reserve Police Force
DIA	–	Defence Intelligence Agency
DU	–	Delhi University
FSB	–	Federal Security Service
HQ	–	Head Quarters
IB	–	Intelligence Bureau
KGB	–	Komitet Gosudarstvennoy Bezopasnosti
MAC address	–	Media Access Control address
MFS	–	Ministry for State Security
NSA	–	National Security Agency
NTRO	–	National Technical Research Organisation
NGO	–	Non Governmental Organization

NSCN (K)	–	National Socialist Council of Nagaland (Kahaplang)
PM	–	Prime Minister
PMO	–	Prime Minister's Office
POK	–	Pakistan Occupied Kashmir
POW	–	Prisoner of War
RAW	–	Research and Analysis Wing
RBP	–	Reserve Bank of Pakistan
SAVAK	–	Sazeman-e Ettela'at va Amniyat-e Keshvar
ULFA	–	United Liberation Front of Assam